A MAN AT WAR

JOHNNY MAINS

INTRODUCTION BY
CHARLIE HIGSON

PRAISE FOR *A MAN AT WAR*

"A tale that is as brutal and chilling as it is elegantly told. Mains is at the top of his game and in Russell Stickles has created a unique and compellingly deviant protagonist."
—Lucie McKnight Hardy, author of *Dead Relatives* and *Water Shall Refuse Them*

"Johnny Mains takes us into disturbed minds – long after you've finished reading them, you can still hear them – he is a truly underrated writer who will haunt you."
—Robin Ince, author of *Bibliomaniac*

"Mains' writing in A Man at War *is like a bullet to the brain, a shock to the system. It's not just that he is a master of narrative tension and pace – which he is – but he is constantly surprising you, making you wonder what the hell is going to happen next."*
—Reggie Oliver, author of *A Maze for the Minotaur, and Other Strange Stories*

"Mains' willingness to let the story go where it wants is quite remarkable and refreshing."
—Ralph Robert Moore, author of *Behind You*

"Russell Stickles is a terrifically ugly character, and Mains has created a deeply uneasy tale in which the familiar and the fantastical collide."
—Tim Major, author of *Hope Island*

"Johnny Mains' writing always sports a quirky, engaging and idiosyncratic character."
—Barry Forshaw, *Crime Time*

*This book is dedicated to Lucie McKnight Hardy
who told me to keep going.*

*And to the memory of Peter Straub:
"You do not reject the supernatural out of hand."*

CONTENTS

Introduction by Charlie Higson: XI

The Cut (1957-1959): 1

Choke (1986): 87

A Man at War (1941-1942): 157

Afterword by Johnny Mains: 233

INTRODUCTION

CHARLIE HIGSON

"While I find comfort in books, I sometimes feel that as I have devoted the last thirty years to creating them, they now own whatever remains of my soul. I will never be able to escape them."

THIS IS A book about books. About stories, stories within stories, about writers (both real and fictional) and editors, about bookshops and collectors and libraries, about secrets and lies, and how the horrors of the real world invade and colonise our fictional worlds – and vice versa. The quote above, spoken in the book by its monstrous protagonist, Russell Stickles, could equally well apply to its author, the wonderful – and not at all monstrous – Johnny Mains. Particularly if you replace the word "creating" with "collecting".

I first met Johnny Mains when he interviewed me about my YA horror series, *The Enemy*. One of a series of events he'd organised at an Arts Centre in Plymouth. As a fellow horror fanatic, I was immensely impressed by the depth and breadth of his knowledge. Not just about the history of fictional horror – the stories, writers, directors, actors, publishers, musicians – from the 18th century to the present day, but also the real-life historical figures who fed into and influenced so much of this world, from Vlad the Impaler to Ed Gein. This was no dilettante. It was clear that Johnny had done a deep dive into horror and was still enthusiastically exploring its murky depths looking for rotting corpses.

After our event he showed me the comprehensive collection of books, DVDs, tapes, magazines, artefacts and ephemera he'd collected over the years, and I was impressed all over again. He was particularly proud of his complete collection of *Pan Books of Horror* that had done so much to revive and perpetuate the genre in their heyday of the '60s and '70s. The series was created (and initially edited) by Herbert van Thal in 1959, and it ran to thirty volumes, finally going to its unquiet grave in 1989. The cheap paperbacks, with their lurid covers promising much transgressive sex and violence, were the gateway to horror for many teenagers of my generation. Amassing a set also holds a strong attraction to the male collecting instinct, to which Johnny is not immune.

I paid homage to Johnny and his collection in a story I wrote for one of his anthologies (*Dead Funny*). It was about a faded horror movie icon meeting an obsessive fan and being shown round their collection. As the story progresses, it becomes clear that one of them is a vampire – but which one? They're both feeding off each other, locked into that mutually dependant relationship so familiar to anyone who's ever attended a fantasy and horror convention.

Johnny started as a horror fan, and then became an obsessive collector, before, finally, longing to add to the world he loved, he became an editor, battling to revive the Pan horror imprint as well as putting together his own anthologies – both of new writing and old forgotten works. And then, inevitably, he became an author in his own right. With his books now sitting on the shelves alongside his heroes. But he still loves to edit anthologies. He still obsessively scours the archives, delighted when he turns up a lost gem.

So knowledgeable is he, so well researched, that I once said, only half-jokingly, that he should be made Minister of Horror. He loves the world, and gives so much to it, but it's a world of corruption and decay, of cruelty and pain, of illness and darkness and death, so he couldn't possibly spend a lifetime immersed in it without being touched by it. How else could he so well understand the terrible Russell Stickles, who can't escape his awful and bloody past? Stickles is surrounded always by the ghosts of those he's done wrong to, while Johnny's surrounded by all that he's collected. And every book is surely haunted by the ghost of its dead author . . .

I don't think Amicus ever made a portmanteau horror film centred around a mad book collector and the stories in his haunted library, but they should have done. With the unhinged collector played by Peter Cushing, or Patrick Magee, or Johnny Mains . . . Because horror fiction has always revolved around books and texts, often found hidden – in an attic or a trunk, or a locked archive. So many classic works – from *Frankenstein*, to *Dracula*, *Dr Jekyll and Mr Hyde*, and on to *Carrie* and *The Blair Witch Project* – are presented in the form of a collection of letters, diary extracts, secret journals, newspaper clippings, found video footage . . . As if the authors are saying – "this isn't fantasy, I didn't make this up, it's all real . . ."

It's no surprise that such a well-read fan as Johnny Mains would use this trope in his own work. For him the books, the texts, or at least the ownership of them, are almost the most important thing. Stickles himself is prepared to kill to protect his own flimsy 'authorship', having stolen the work of a dead rival and passed it off as his own. It's this act of literary vampirism that cements his success as an author. He'd love to be a truly great one, but he knows he's no literary genius. We get to see pieces of some of his numerous attempts at writing in the book. Whether it's a journal, an extract from an aborted children's book, or references to the one modest novel he actually wrote – and the other one that he stole.

Alongside the fictional Stickles we get to meet a host of real-life authors. And they're carefully chosen. Among them are Robert Aickman (upon whom Stickles is very loosely based), the aforementioned Herbert van Thal (for obvious reasons), and perhaps most tellingly, Dennis Wheatley, the astonishingly successful British author who straddled and combined the worlds of historical fiction, science fiction, spy fiction, the occult and the supernatural. And in real life worked for the secret service during the war.

Elements of the work of all three of these authors suffuse *A Man at War*. Dennis Wheatley provides Johnny with a way into the world of spies, and a model for mixing genres. Herbert van Thal represents the horrific violence, gore and sheer nastiness of many of the Pan stories (particularly in later volumes), and it's the weird, unsettling, small town world of Aickman that provides our milieu. Aickman managed to subvert mundane, stifling, boring, grey, little England with an atmosphere of dread and the uncanny that was entirely his own. He's the Philp Larkin of horror and to my mind is our greatest and most chilling horror writer. His stories all have a core of unsettling mystery that is often unexplained and, indeed, unexplainable. You come away from reading him with a headache and the nagging feeling that you've missed something. Something important and very dangerous. You're aware of a deeper mystery lying outside the confines of the story, nagging at you, but always remaining beyond your grasp. Johnny has channelled Aickman in this book. He hasn't tried to tidy things up, he's left it messy and often opaque. Certain moments seem to defy explanation. And he's left it to the reader to make their own sense out of the bombed-out building this work is.

Perhaps, when you consider the diverse inspirations for this book, it's unsurprising that *A Man at War* is hard to pin down. Is it a horror story, a psychological thriller, a spy thriller, a historical novel of wartime Britain . . .? No. Surely, it's all of those things and more.

But let's call it horror. Certainly, horrific things happen, and the central character, Russell Stickles is undoubtedly a monster – haunted by the dead he has created. He's a self-justifying murderer, who spreads chaos and mayhem, but always expects the reader to sympathise with him. Constantly beaten, blown up, his bones broken, his skin lacerated, he's a sadomasochistic fiend who always somehow manages to rise from the dead and limp back to wreak more vengeance. He is, indeed ". . . the remains that won't stay in their grave."

Johnny's put his heart and soul, and years of research, into this book, and his love of genre books and their creators jumps out of every page.

He's cooked it all down into a pungent stew, that leaves a strange taste in your mouth. You'll be picking your teeth for days after you finish it . . .

What are you waiting for? Take your first bite.

—**Charlie Higson,**
The Castle of Otranto,
August, 2022

THE CUT

(1957–1959)

"I don't want to get well
For I'm having a wonderful time . . ."
—'I Don't Want to Get Well'
Harry Pease and Howard Johnson

RUSSELL - MOTHER

"I AM THE remains that won't stay in their grave," I whisper to myself as I look in the mirror. I pull the skin from my face. It feels flabby, yields too much. I let go, sigh, walk back into the bedroom, to the drawer, take out a fresh pair of paisley underpants and put them on, trying my hardest not to fall over as I stick a leg in the left hole. I rub my stomach, my hand drifting over the ancient burn marks like a blind person reads braille, frowning at my slight paunch. I can't complain; the last week has been rather extravagant. There have been several trains into London, as many meals as I can handle at Rules in Covent Garden, and then, this evening, a terribly grandiose dining experience at the Criterion, next door to the theatre in Piccadilly.

The Criterion had come about because Mitchell Bird asked me to a showing of *End of Joy*, which he had directed. It wasn't really to my taste, although I hadn't told Mitchell that. It was billed as a farcical comedy, something I would normally be at the front of the queue for, but it was sadly a waste of good talent. The play had been running since June, so it must have had *some* merit and I was confidently told that Gainsborough Pictures were turning it into a film with Eric Pohlmann and Googie Withers. Some devils have all the luck.

I walk to my typewriter and dash off a quick letter:

11.2.57

Mitchell,

I really enjoyed this evening. I thought that End of Joy *was a* real *hoot, I can see why it's been so successful. We must do dinner again soon.*

Cordially yours,

Russell

    I take the paper quickly out from the roller with a *vvvvvvtttt*, fold it into four, put it in a brown envelope and address it to Mitchell at the theatre for convenience. I lick the stamp. I've never minded the glue. It makes my tongue claggy.
    The first stabbing pain in my stomach hits me, followed by a deep, watery gurgle.
    The fish pie.
    Resigned to my fate, I go to the small bookcase and quickly scan its contents and settle on Wharton's *Certain People*. I have been meaning to read it for a while.

It has always been the case that I've felt that my body is breaking down and has been for quite some time; my teeth feel loose and I always seem to have a heavy, metallic feeling in my mouth, something that first started in my late teens.
    I throw up several times, one of which is such a catastrophic event I feel that the end will never come and that this illness is something I will never be able to return from. The book is forgotten, neglected in the bathtub minutes after my first visit. I try to drink a glass of water to

keep myself hydrated, but my hand shakes so badly trying to lift the porcelain cup to my lips. The water comes back up minutes after ingesting, and there is nothing to do but ride it out.

I collapse onto the bed, my body covered in a greasy sheen, my legs kicking out for an invisible purchase every time a malignant torrent of sickness raises its head and consumes me.

"Russell?" a strained cry from my mother's bedroom across the hall. "I need you."

I pause for several seconds while I think of what to do. I can't wake up my wife who is asleep in the room next door, and it's impossible for me to go to see my mother without the possibility of me being sick or worse, in her room.

"It's going to have to wait until morning," I say. I try to keep my voice down as much as possible. I don't want Binky to wake up, I don't want her to fuss me, and-

"It's my heart," my mother wails, and I get up, throw the bedroom door open and there is Binky, my wife, who is one step ahead of me and we enter my mother's room. She is sitting up, the light is on and her face is sallow and grey and she clutches at her left elbow.

"You'll have to go to the pub, wake them up and demand they use their phone," I say to Binky, who nods. She wears a baggy pink chiffon nightdress and her feet are as white as my mother's face.

"Don't worry," I say. I stroke the hair back from my mother's forehead. I have not seen her this scared since the episode during the War. Binky thunders down the stairs, the third stair from the bottom making a more horrendous squeal of protest than usual. My mother looks at me and whispers, "I forgive you." We both know

4

what she means. She then pitches forward, makes a strange grunting noise, like a dog who has been trained to seek out truffles. She then collapses back onto the raised pillows and she is dead.

My breathing is rapid, my own heartbeat skittering in my chest and I think for a moment that I might instantly join her, so I concentrate on a small stain on the wall above her and do my hardest not to look at her chest which is no longer moving. After a while I steal a sly look at her face. It is slack, like a sodden *papier mâché* mask. *This* is death. *This* is the pantomime, and she has exited, stage never-ending darkness.

To be sitting on the edge of the bed with the only dead person I have ever 'loved' is at once discombobulating and freeing. I can say what I want without fear of reproach or rolled eyes. I remain quiet and see that death has given her her final eye roll.

I cough and the cough turns into a sob and I bury my head into her chest and in that act of crying I will everything I have into starting her heart up again, for her to wrap her arms around me and to say that it was just all a silly little trick and that she is fine and nothing's the matter and don't be such a silly little mother's boy.

"You are the remains, you will stay in your grave," I whisper. It's at that moment my mother opens her eyes and fixes them on me. She screams and with her hand that was clutching her elbow, rakes deep furrows into my skin and stuffs what she's grabbed into the greedy mouth with sharp, splintered teeth.

I fall back from the bed, but nothing has happened, my mind has just taken me to one of its strange places again and my mother is quite dead and I wait for Binky to return, but don't want to be with my mother any longer so I make my way downstairs to the kitchen, when another bolt of fish revenge hits me and I soil myself.

I am in bed. The doctor has given me a draught of several medicinal wares, one to relax the grip of food poisoning, the other a mind relaxant, to dull the sensations that I am or am supposed to be feeling. I don't really know what is happening. Binky is being kind and she sits at the end of the bed, talking to me about how I don't need to do anything, she'll wash and dress mother and have her laid out for visitors. I tell her that I don't really want anyone to come round, but she chides me to not be so silly, people will want to pay their respects.

Your mother was a well-liked woman.

I don't want to fight, but neither do I want to give in. The medicine forces my hand and I drift off into unknown seas.

People are very nice to you when your loved ones die. They always say things they don't mean. Promises of this, that and the other; were you to ever follow them up you would surely be met with looks of horror and hasty excuses. This time is no different and when Mr Frankfort Arnold, an old publisher friend of my father's, shakes my hand and asks if there is anything he can do, that I need only place a call, I instantly take him up on his offer.

"I've finished writing a novel. Will you read it?"

Confusion floods his face; it is of course the last thing he would ever expect to be asked at such a solemn occasion; it is of course a vulgar thing to ask. He lets go of my hand and nods in defeated agreement. I tell him to wait and I leave him in the reception room, surrounded by the mourning and the curious. I run upstairs to the bedroom and take a copy of the manuscript, one of six, tied together with twine, and go back downstairs and hand it over to him. He promises me he'll read it and leaves not long after.

The rest of the day is good. The sandwiches are tolerable even if they are only paste and cucumber. Binky is being Binky, birdlike Binky, trying to make her presence felt whilst simultaneously trying to be invisible. Sometimes she pulls it off and when she does it is a most remarkable thing to see. Magicians would pay thousands for her secret.

I am going to make love to her tonight. We have moved back into the same room. Mother's room is the place for this fresh start. The bed that belonged to mother has been taken outside and burned. There is no question of anyone ever lying upon that bed again. I also want to remove the wallpaper, the insipid green and orange floral pattern makes me queasy. I find that if I stare at it too long I feel as if I am being carried out to sea, the flowers start to sway and swirl and curl in on themselves until I snap myself away.

The room is full of smoke, even though only one or two people are puffing away. Someone has put fresh coal on the fire, coal mixed in with soot that was in the bucket. Binky has to get everyone out while I deal with the fiery aftermath. I try to breathe as little as I can. The chatter of everyone out on the street filters in. I can only begin to think about what the neighbours are saying, the ones that never really liked my mother, although they would never have said that to her face during her life. Although cowed by certain life events, and perhaps due to them, when need be, her tongue was sharper than a gutting knife.

RUSSELL - HUNG

I EJACULATE INTO the toilet bowl. I watch my semen string. All at once I feel empty. I yank the heavy chain, pull up my underpants, unlock the door and go back through to the bedroom where Binky is lying on the bed, her eyes closed. She is naked and still. I dress silently, not looking at her. She never lets me enjoy her to completion.

"Will you pick up some meat from the butcher after your trip to the library?" she asks gently. Her voice startles me, she is normally quite quiet for the rest of the day after our attempts at full copulation. Perhaps she is surprised that this is the third time I have worshipped between her legs in a week.

"Of course, what would you like me to get?"

"Some lamb, some tripe, some skirt, oh...and maybe a bone so I can make soup."

I take my blazer from the wardrobe, check that my bifold wallet is there, put on my spectacles and go back to Binky and kiss her gently on the lips. She still doesn't move.

I like to walk. I walk as often as I can, in all sorts of weather. Today it is muggy and I wish I didn't have to wear my blazer but one has appearances to keep. It wouldn't do for people to see the sweat marks on my shirt. The street is quiet, Mr and Mrs Gently wave at me as they turn the corner onto our road, they have probably been at the social club, yes of course, it is Tuesday, that is their day.

I think about Mother as I walk to the library. I never had the luxury of a father when I was a child. He was killed in Ypres, he took a bullet to the eye. His friend fished the slug out and sent it to Mother after the war was over. I have no idea why, but that kind act made it into my novel, it is too good of a thing to let vanish into the ether, the world must know that this is what men do.

Mother never liked Binky, even less when she had to move in with us. Binky was immediately reduced to a wilting wallflower. I do believe that my mother killed off her spirit, as mother's are wont to do with the rivals for their son's affections. It could have been her revenge against that long shadow of Doreen, who she met during the War. A strange thing, but mother completely ignored Binky before she became ill and had to move in with us. She was more than happy in her house, pottering away, playing bridge with her many friends, all who seemed slowly to ebb away and forget about her the more ill she became.

Bones for soup. An old habit that Binky of course got from *her* mother, also deceased. Bones to flavour vegetable soup. The mind boggles. A car drives past me, and I don't care to see who it is. The car is unfamiliar. It stops just in front. A man gets out and I try not to look at him, but he says "Russell," and I recognise the voice immediately.

Frankfort Arnold, publisher.

"Ah!" I wait for him to step onto the pavement before shaking his hand.

"I have just been to your house, there was no answer."

I nod, Binky would still be lying on the bed, understanding that I may want to worship her on my return. I do not tell Frankfort this, of course.

"Anyway," Frankfort continues, "I want to talk to you about your manuscript. Can we drive somewhere?"

"I am going to the library, there is a pub nearby, The Sedentary Falcon, you know of it?"

"Yes."

The drive is pleasant, Frankfort does not talk about the novel, instead he talks to me about my father, and how they used to play, as teens together on the Stour, catching newts and tadpoles in jars. I am frustrated. I want to mention the manuscript, but I am polite and I know I have to bide my time.

The beer is warm. I wish I had ordered a whisky instead. I take polite sips. I intend to not drink the whole pint.

The handle is too small for my hand to fit comfortably.

"Russell, this could be a *great* book," Frankfort says, staring at me intently. "At the moment it is merely a good book."

"I see."

"I *will* work with you to make it a great book. Are you aware of Gerald Humap?"

"No."

"He's one of the best editors in the business. He will help shape your book into something beautiful. Are you willing to put in the work?"

"Yes, yes of course."

"Good." Frankfort grins.

I am slightly merry and decide not to go to the library. I do not want to choose a book while under the influence. I would get most disheartened if I chose incorrectly and have to make a return visit.

The butcher, Mr Gatler, is welcoming and prepares most of my request.

"We will get someone to deliver a few good bones tomorrow. Andrew Rubbard took the last few for his dogs."

"Very well, how much do I owe you?"

The walk home is pleasant; from the butcher's you have to walk up Sommernacht Hill, the name a Germanic throwback that the locals tried, but failed to have removed in the year after the war ended – past the doctor's surgery, the police station and then into the park, following the lazy path out to the other side and onto Widdershins Lane, crossing over by the school and making your way down Match Road before turning left and you arrive at Dottage Villas, where you will find my house, No. 36. The garden is tidy and I smile at the roses under the window.

The door is locked so I open it, balancing the butcher's meat in one arm, and I am greeted by Binky; well, Binky's mottled feet. She has hanged herself from the bannister.

I walk through the piss on the floor and to the kitchen, looking up at her as I pass, she is still naked. I put the meat in the mesh racking in the larder, no rat could break into it no matter how hard they tried.

I put a pan of water on the cream New World 42 cooker, turn the gas on and light it with a match. The gas catches and makes a lovely *whoomph.*

"Cup of tea, Binky?" I shout.

I hear a creak, but that is, of course, the weight of her body pulling down on the rope.

"The butcher didn't have any bones, they'll be delivered tomorrow," I continue. My voice has a *slight* strain to it.

I turn the burner off and go to the drawer and pull out a bread knife. I look at it and decide that it should saw through the rope quite capably.

I go up the stairs, leaving wet footprints, ducking past Binky's small circular movements, and when I reach the top, walk to where she tied the rope. I saw through it easily. Binky is free, she lands with a discourteous thump. I go downstairs, walk over Binky's awkward corpse and put the knife back in its rightful place. I pick Binky up. She is surprisingly hefty. I carry her up the stairs and lay her on the bed, and slowly dress her in her favourite pink chiffon nightgown. I move her over to my side of the bed while I pull back the blankets, and roll her back in, struggling slightly as I try to sit her up.

I go through to the small bookcase in the other room and decide on *The Man in Control* by Charles McGraw, a story about a man who marries a woman only to find out that she is frigid and her tastes lie with other women. I place the book in her hands and leave her be.

RUSSELL - EMBERS

I MAKE MY way to my local pub, which isn't The Sedentary Falcon, but a much more tasteful place called The Hardy Knight. It is early, but the landlady, a matronly type with beefy hands that are useful at closing time, welcomes me warmly and tells me that she'll bring over my drink. I have brought a book with me, Ngaio Marsh's *The Scales of Justice*, and I open it and scan the first couple of pages idly, sighing at the name of the village, Swevenings.

The landlady brings over my beer, it has a frothy head. I give her a couple of coins, she is pleased that there's a tip in there for her. I take a long deep drink, relishing the bitterness of burnt hops.

I think about Frankfort. It was good of him to drive back to Effingham so soon after my mother's funeral and the fact that the book certainly holds so much promise is a testament to my natural talent. I'm not too pleased with the fact that it needs work. I think the book is perfect as it is and I shudder as I recall the words "a second, maybe a third draft is needed." I do not think it will come to that. The Editor will see that the book doesn't need that much work.

I drink my beer.

In due course someone comes rushing into the pub and asks if they've seen me. The pub is much busier by this time. I am still at the table, sitting alone, the book closed as it isn't grabbing me as much as I hope it would.

I am told that my house is on fire. I say that my wife is in the house. The noise in the pub lowers. We all know that there isn't a fire service in Effingham, the nearest being in Haven, thirteen miles away. Several buildings in the town have fallen victim recently, but the horrors of the war are still fresh in everyone's mind and the memories of losing most of the village of Hobbs End, half a mile away, to the Luftwaffe's bombs. It reminds me of the lodgings I once inhabited in London.

There is nothing to be done. The house is razed. I hear someone say that it's a good thing that it's a detached house. I think about all of the things that I owned which are now destroyed. I will need a new typewriter. The Rector arrives on the scene and he tells me that I can stay at the Rectory for as long as is needed. I nod my thanks. The village policeman, Artie Stein, asks me a couple of questions. Binky took to bed with a glass of sherry, she was feeling . . . emotional, what with the recent events. She liked to read by candlelight. Artie nods in agreement and puts his hand on my shoulder and says if there is anything I need . . .

There is a group of about fifty of us watching the smoke billow up into the sky, thinking about dead Binky and wondering when the fire engine will arrive. Children cycle up and down the street, shouting at each other about being on fire, their hair speckled with ash.

I wake up. The unfamiliar bed has given me backache. I put on a dressing gown, loaned to me by the Rector and I make my way across oak flooring to the bedroom door which is on a simple latch. It clicks loudly as it lifts and I fear that I will wake the household. I tread to the other end of the landing where the bathroom is. I urinate for over a minute in one urgent stream. The green bathroom makes me shudder and I wonder how the tile-makers manage to make their tiles such a purulent colour. Should I flush? That will wake up the household. I flush, with the lid down. It is nearly seven.

The toast is dry. The Rector's wife scrimps on the margarine. The tea is hot and sweet. Their daughter comes in, a girl of thirteen. She barely glances at me, sits down and picks up a slice of toast.

"So you're the one who lost his wife in the fire," she says, taking a small, perfect bite.

"Don't be so *rude*, Angela!" the Rector's wife barks, her wattle red with embarrassment.

"She's not lost, she's dead," I reply, knowing what I'm saying but it has the desired effect; Angela looks at me as if I am crazy and decides I'm not worth talking to.

The Rector enters, his cuffs flapping. "Have you seen my cufflinks?" he asks his wife.

They are gold. I have put one in separate trouser pockets so they do not clink together when I walk.

"Can I use your telephone, I need to place a call with my publisher." The words sound grand when they come out of my mouth and the Rector immediately takes me through to the table by the bottom of the staircase. I lift up the receiver and after a couple of seconds the operator arrives and I ask her to ring Knightsbridge 612. The call is connected and I ask the secretary if Mr Arnold is there. I am told to wait a minute. That is fine. I am not paying for the call.

"Russell! You've not had any second thoughts have you?"

"No, I just thought it prudent to inform you that last night the house went up in flames and Binky perished."

"Good *God*."

I can hear the shock, the fright in his voice. It makes the line crackle.

"Where are you?"

"I'm at the Rectory. The Rector has kindly put me up. I have to make an appointment with the insurance company and they will have to come, but I thought it was only courteous . . ."

"I will send a car round to pick you up this afternoon. You can stay with me, all insurance companies are based in London anyway and we can travel back up for the funeral. When will that be?"

"A week today. It will be a closed casket, of course."

"Of course. You poor, poor man. I'll see you later." He hangs up the phone. I do the same and I go back up the stairs to my room. I close the door behind me and sit on the borrowed bed.

A knock on my door. The Rector, his face apologetic. "There's someone here to see you, I tried to send her away, but she insisted . . ." He leaves the last word hanging in the air and I think of Binky and how I checked the rope for blood after I had removed it from her neck and frayed the end of the rope where I cut so as to not make it look too neat before taking it to the shed and placing it behind a petroleum can.

I walk downstairs, I like how my weight feels on the staircase, the wood gives ever so slightly but doesn't squeak.

Gemima is waiting, sitting very upright in a chair that must have been brought back from the church. I say that I am happy to see her. She throws herself onto me and starts to sob. I pat her back gently and after a while she releases me and I have a wet patch on my blazer from her tears.

"Poor, poor Binky," she wails. They were childhood friends. It appears that Binky has never told Gemima about our interior secrets and that is for the good. I am looked at with nothing but love and sorrow.

"I walked past your house this morning, it is still smoking. Cigarette?" she asks, unaware of her *faux pas*, pulling out a slim silver case from her day purse.

"Not here, the Rector wouldn't approve."

RUSSELL - BOOK

I AM NERVOUS. I am assured that everything will be fine. I am in Foyles on Charing Cross Road, staring at a whole wall of my book, *An Uneasy Dream*. I *feel* as if I am in a dream. I am holding a glass of champagne which I'm loath to sip; there will be many people surrounding me in less than an hour. Frankfort doesn't look nervous, in fact he is positively beaming.

"There will be a review coming in the *Times Literary Supplement* and you have absolutely nothing to worry about, I can quote verbatim, 'as important a writer as Graham Greene.'"

My heart swells. My brain sings. I am an *important* author.

People are swirling round me. I don't like shaking hands. I feel that my handshake isn't strong enough, but it is all right, everyone else's handshakes are equally limp. I am introduced to a growlingly ugly man, smoking a cheroot. His lips are chapped. I nudge my spectacles up on my nose.

"Russell, meet Herbert van Thal, he's currently putting together a volume of strange stories for Pan Books."

"Call me Bertie, please," he says in one of the softer London accents, taking my hand and crushing it. He has shark eyes. They are fixed on me.

"Frankfort sent me an advanced copy of your book a couple of months ago. I have to say, it's a most remarkable work. Sublime." He breathes quickly, like a tramp with a found shilling. He continues apace; "So, Russell Stickles, do you have an agent? I would love you to write a story or two for some anthologies I have upcoming, I have one, *The Pan Book of Horror Stories*, coming out next December if you can write a story for it?" Still, his stare. He is hungry for my words.

Someone pats me on the shoulder. I spin around and there is Binky, burnt and blackened Binky. She opens her mouth and dirty grey smoke drifts out, mingling in with the smoke of the party. She touches my hand. I blink. Binky is gone. It is not Binky. It is a young woman. Alive. Breathing. Skin unblemished by flame. She is a violence of beauty.

EMILIA - SIGNED

I PAT HIS shoulder and he spins round, the abrupt suddenness of it shocking us both. I immediately smile. It appeases him. His heavy spectacles frame a face that looks drawn.

"Russell Stickles?"

"Yes?"

"I'm Emilia. Emilia Goldstone. I just want to take a second to say how much I love your book, it's moved me incredibly." I touch his hand gently.

He looks shocked, then smiles out of politeness and it lights up his face. He steps to one side and introduces me to an editor called Bertie who looks me up and down and wolfishly agrees with my attire. We small-talk for a while and then Frankfort Arnold arrives with loud aplomb, kisses my cheek and takes Russell away where he is paraded around like a showpony. He looks slightly dazed.

Frankfort has already told me all about Russell and what happened to his wife. I look at him as he sits down at a table and people take copies of his book for him to sign. I get my own copy, pay for it and wait patiently in the queue while waiters and waitresses bring out trays of champagne and small snacks. After five minutes or so it is my turn to have a book signed. He smiles at me again and asks what I would like, flatsigned or dedication.

"Dedication, please."

To Emilia Goldstone – who likes this book so much she now has two *copies, the one without my signature surely worth more. With my warmest thanks, Russell Stickles, 15/4/58*

He passes me back my book and I look at the inscription.

"Were you given your first copy by Frankfort?" he asks.

"Yes, he and my father are friends and he makes a habit of sending me uncorrected proofs of upcoming novels. It's no lie when I say that your book has deeply affected me, it's quite unlike any other."

This pleases him greatly.

"When I am next in London, I would like to take you out for a meal."

"That would be lovely," I say, as he reaches out and touches my hand. My stomach flips lightly.

RUSSELL - TYPE

I MAKE MY way back to Effingham on the train. In my suitcase there are several copies of my book. At the station I am met by the Rector who hugs me and we drive a pleasant mile to the cottage I am renting on the outskirts of the village. The place is called Clemendy. It has electricity but no running water; that I have to pump by hand from the well outside. The Rector comes in for a cup of tea and I give him a copy of my book. He asks me to sign it, which I do, of course.

To the Reverend Graham Roberts, a dear friend who helped me during a time of great personal crisis. With my warmest thanks, the author, 16/4/1958

He stays for slightly longer than I want him to. He asks me all about my time in London, the launch, the connections I have made and about the British Library, a place he has always meant to go and visit but has never found the time to, what with the needs of the busy parish.

After he leaves I go to the cooker and I cook myself a pork chop and some potatoes. I drown the food in gravy. I take my plate to the table by the window and eat, listening to the evening birdsong. Once I wash up I make my way to the toilet and I ejaculate into the toilet bowl, thinking about Emilia Goldstone's green eyes and curly brown hair.

I roll a fresh sheet into the typewriter. It is morning. I am naked, the curtains are drawn. My fingers punch the keys hard and before long I drift into the rhythm of writing.

Anne (I am unsure if that was her given name, she went by many) was sitting at the table worrying at the fingernail of her ring finger. She knew that if she bit down it would bleed and be sore for days. A waiter came up to her, an exotic type whose eyebrows were thick and black as pitch. He asked her if she would like her glass refilled. She nodded, yes.

It is lunch and I have typed roughly two thousand words. Bertie says he would like three to five thousand and that is something that I should be able to do by the end of the day. I am finding that the words are flowing through me evenly, not in fits and starts like when my mother and Binky were around. There are now no more interruptions to my life and I am able to type when I see fit. A letter is pushed through the letterbox and I give it a slight glance as I go upstairs, urinate and get dressed into a pair of slacks and a shirt with short sleeves. Binky lies on the bed, her legs spread. She smiles as I look at her; I think it is a smile, her face is too badly burnt to correctly tell, but her teeth are showing, they are unusually white.

"Fuck me," she whispers. Her vocal chords are too damaged to produce anything louder.

My mother stands by the side of the bed, chuckling. "Yes, fuck her," mother says, stroking the hairless head of Binky. There is nothing wrong with *her* voice.

I am sweating. I am not feverish. I have moved a wardrobe from the spare room up against the main bedroom door so I can no longer enter it. It has taken me an hour to move the solid oak monstrosity.

I sit at the typewriter, but my concentration has been broken. I decide to go to a pub. It is called The Willows. The envelope is left on the floor, awaiting my return. Once there I discover I have left my bifold wallet in the blocked-up bedroom. I walk back home.

Once I have retrieved my wallet from the room and the wardrobe is back in its place, I stare at the envelope that is on the floor. I pick it up, a lovely cream colour. The writing on the envelope is in block, a vulgar way to address a letter. I make my way to the table, pick up my letter opener.   I have to use more than a little force to open the envelope; the opener either · needs sharpening or the envelope is made out of a particularly heavy grain.

The writing contained is thankfully not block, but elegant and flowing:

22.4.58

Dear Russell,
I would like to say what a pleasure it was meeting you last week at your book launch. It's a shame (for me) that it was so busy and I wasn't able to talk to you as much as I would have liked. I hope you do not mind me writing to you like this, I asked Frankfort for your address, he told me that you have no telephone.
I don't want you to simply think of me as a silly woman fawning over you, I meant what I said – that your book touched me deeply, it grabbed hold of my soul from the moment I read

the first paragraph and your words are still to let me go . . .

I finish the letter, all six pages of it, leaving it on the table and walk the half mile to the pub and order myself a whisky instead of my traditional beer. I need something stronger after today. After it is finished I order another and another.

The walk home is slow. The sun is slowly settling down for the night and the woods on either side of me are silent. I sing.

You made me want you
And all the time you knew it
I guess you always knew it

I stumble at the front door and drop the key. I pick it up and sway as I try to enter the house. The armchair calls me.

I finish the story. It is called 'An Incurable Ability'. I spend the rest of the day typing out two more copies, both on carbon.

Once I have finished for the day I fold up one copy of the story and put it into an envelope and address it, Herbert van Thal (Editor), % Weidenfeld and Nicolson, 7 Cork Street, London, W1. I place the envelope on the mantelpiece. I make myself a cold beef sandwich and a cup of tea for dinner. I finish reading *Twilight Stories* by Rhoda Broughton, a book that was published by Bertie under his Home and van Thal imprint ten years before.

When it is time I take the blankets from the cupboard, sit on the chair and close my eyes.

EMILIA - EFFINGHAM

THE CARRIAGE I am in is crowded, but everyone is reading so I do not feel too overwhelmed by curious looks. I brush back my hair when it falls over my eyes and I remonstrate with myself for not bringing a headband with me. The ticket collector stares at my crossed legs when he comes in, I chastise him with my eyes.

The journey from Liverpool Street is quite a pleasant one, the Essex countryside giving way to the Stour Valley, the Ellis Hills and eight stops until the train pulls in at Effingham, a station that you have to request to stop at. If you neglect to tell anyone at the start of your journey you are stuck on the train until you arrive at Loudun, the biggest town up the line. The station at Effingham used to have a splinter track that would take you to Haven and Mercy, but has been abandoned ever since the War. All of this I have read about in guides.

When the ticket inspector yells "Effingham." I get up, reach up to the luggage rack and pull down my small satchel. Two men stand to let me past and I open the carriage door just as the train slowly halts. I slide the door window down and reach for the handle and open the door myself before the platform inspector reaches me. I see annoyance flash across his face. I lightly jump off the train and I see Russell near the newspaper stand. I wave at him. He waves back and begins to take a step forward which he rescinds as soon as he sees the amount of people getting off the train. I make my way towards him and I see that he has had a haircut and in the months since we last met he has lost some weight. It is pleasing to see, it makes his once doughy face more of a delight to study.

"Hello Emilia," he says warmly, proffering his hand.

"Don't be silly." I reach up and kiss him on the lips. He colours and looks around him to see who has noticed.

"I'm sorry I haven't come down to London recently," he says, "I caught a stupid cold and then, as you know, I broke my wrist."

His letters to me have been suffused with sadness for some time. He complained of not being able to type properly and it taking him much longer to write anything of note. It had given him, he explained, much more time for inward reflection, and in those letters he told me that he loved me as much as I loved him.

He takes my satchel and we make our way out of the station and walk into the village, admiring gardens and one bold houseowner who had painted their place peach. We stop at a cafe and order a cream tea and we talk about my journey and what books I have been sent by Frankfort.

After the tea we walk to the River Stour and by the ruins of the old Mill. There is a new bridge, replaced by the Mill Trust. I kiss Russell properly for the first time. My tongue searches for and touches his and he reels back with shock.

"I'm sorry," he says, "nobody has ever kissed me like this before."

We kiss again. A magpie cackles in the trees behind us and we break apart from each other and laugh.

I brush my knees free from dirt and straighten my skirt and take Russell by the hand. He kisses me.

"I can taste . . ." he starts to say but he is interrupted by the sight of another couple walking through the woods.

"Oh no," he moans, taking his hand and rubbing his forehead frantically.

"Russell? Is that really you?" A woman, maybe fifteen, twenty years older than myself walks down the path towards us, several steps ahead of her male companion. "How strange to find you down here! And who is this?"

"Hello Gemima," Russell says mechanically. Gemima envelops him in a deep cuddle. He gets out of it as quickly as he can. "This," he says, "is Emilia. We met at the launch party of my book. She is visiting for the day."

Gemima studies me carefully, notices the mottled blemishes on my knees and her face hardens. "Hello Emilia, how lovely to meet you. You've been taking care of him?" It is more of a statement than a question and we both know it.

RUSSELL - RESPONSE

UNTITLED - FIRST DRAFT
Russell Stickles

1.
THE STAINS

Maybe, just maybe, there was a way out of this, Johann Holtzer thought as he fled through the forest, the spruce branches whipping at his face. His boots were so heavy with claggy mud he was tempted to remove them and keep fleeing, but if he was lucky enough to survive the next couple of hours he didn't want his feet to be troublesome for the rest of his days. His father had fought in the first war and had been afflicted with the horror of trench foot. The memories of him reclining, smoking a pipe, barefoot, were as strong as those of recently culled friends.

Johann tripped and fell into the bracken. A rocket or some other explosive device went off nearby, above a cloak of thick white powder. He grappled for his gas mask and frantically put it on. He reached for his rifle and slowly got back up to his feet, continuing to make his way through the dense trees, trying to become one with the deep shadows of the forest . . .

I STOP FOR the night. I count my output, one and a half thousand words. I am pleased. I pick up a pile of mail, sent to me via my publisher. Fan letters. I make myself a cup of tea. I own a kettle now, and this makes me incredibly happy, although the whistle it makes does annoy me.

Dear Russell,

I am writing to you with regards to your debut novel The Uncanny Dream . . .

Dear Sir,

My wife bought me a copy of your book, An Uneasy Dream *and I have to admit, I was completely blindsided by it. The way that you manage to create such a . . .*

Lieber Herr Stickles,
Ich heiße Petra Schmidt aus Berlin. Es tut mir leid, dass ich kein Englisch sprechen kann. Vielleicht könnten Sie diesen Brief übersetzen lassen? Ihr Buch, Der Unheimliche Traum, *hat die literarischen Kreise hier absolut in Brand gesetzt, und es ist sogar die Rede davon, Sie in Zukunft einzuladen . . .*

Dear 'author',
Your 'book' is a piece of shit . . .

I am angry. Angry at the last letter, which has been ripped up into tiny pieces and flushed down the toilet. Binky is sitting in the chair, rasping at me. I scream as loud as I can, I have no fear of anyone hearing me, the nearest house is two fields away and the stone of the cottage is so thick you could let off a hand grenade in the fireplace and it wouldn't be heard. I punch my head, then punch the wall, angry, pathetic outbursts but there is no other way to deal with it. I know I am a great author, an important author. Why has this letter from this nothing person, this dribble of pond scum, got to me so much?

"They have seen into your soul. You revealed too much in your book," Binky croaks.

"Shut up! Shut up! Shut up!"

"It's so true!" mother yells with glee. "Why did you put yourself out there like that? Little by little the praise will dry up and more and more people will . . ."

I run through to the kitchen and grab a pruning knife. I hold it up to my wrist.

"I'll do it!"

That stops them.

I push the tip of the knife into my skin, a bubble of blood forms around the blade. A dribble runs free and lands on the floor.

"No!"

I pull the knife away, drop it into the sink and run my wrist under the cold water tap, watching as the water splashing into the sink turns pink.

EMILIA - SERVICE

THE TRAIN IS late, delayed by up to half an hour, the platform manager informs me. I smile and walk to a bench where I sit and wait. I thought back to last night and the phone call that Russell made. He had walked all of the way to the Rectory, the other side of Effingham in the pouring rain.

His voice was trembling, I was unsure if this was because of the exertion.

"Can I come and see you?"

He steps off the train, carrying a suitcase and umbrella. Rain is forecast over the next couple of days. I run to him and as we kiss, several people stare at us. One woman mutters "disgusting" close enough to be within earshot. We chatter excitedly and walk to the Hackney and Russell places his luggage in the front storage and we jump in the back. He puts his hand on my knee as the driver asks where we are going.

"Claridges, please" Russell replies.

We drive past the British Museum on our way into Mayfair. As the cab pulls up at the entrance, a doorman takes Russell's suitcase. The cab makes off, and we gaze up at the building, impressed at its beauty.

The hotel's interior is glamorous, like something from a Hollywood movie. A heavy crystal chandelier, easily over one hundred years old welcomes us, glinting whenever light hits it. The Foyer, straight ahead, is busy, residents and visitors having afternoon tea. The suitcase is given to a porter who waits patiently by the side of the reception as Russell checks in and is handed the key for the room.

The porter leads the way up the grand staircase to the first floor and down to the far end of a corridor that seems to last forever. There are Victorian prints on the walls, mainly exotic foliage. Arriving at the room the porter puts down the bag, asks for the key and unlocks the door and takes the suitcase into the room. He places it by the foot of the bed, returns the key and stands still, hands behind his back, as Russell fumbles in his pocket for the appropriate tip. The porter smiles broadly and gives me a side glance as he exits, closing the door behind him. I take the key from Russell's hand and lock the door, the bolt landing with a pleasing 'clunk'.

Russell is lying on the bed. I slowly take off his trousers, he lifts himself up to make it easier for me. He is wearing paisley underpants and his penis is straining against them. He kicks his trousers off when I have them round his feet and they fall to the floor, the remnants of his change spilling out. I unbutton his shirt. His skin, as he warned me, is covered in a mass of white scar tissue, so white. His small paunch is comforting. He takes his shirt off and I notice a bandage on his wrist.

"What's that?"

"Kitchen accident."

I tug down his underpants, his penis springs free. I take him with my hand and climb onto him, guiding as he enters me for our very first time. The hem of my summer dress covers his unruly pubic hair.

"I've never had anyone on top before," he moans, trying not to look at me. I lean forward, pushing down hard on him. My right hand grasps his throat and I squeeze. His head snaps back and his eyes meet mine, full of panic. He tries to push me off, but I squeeze again, harder and rub his lips with my free finger. He opens his mouth slightly and I slide my finger in, pressing down on his tongue. He tries to suck on it and attempts to thrust deeper into me. I choke him hard, and he understands who I am and who I can be for him. His legs twitch; his breathing becomes heavier. He is near. I push down again on his throat, his airway completely closed. He is a stroke or two away and as he orgasms I let go of his throat and arch back as my own rips through me. His eyes roll back into their sockets.

"Oh Emilia," he breathes once he calms down a little. He pulls me to him and kisses me. "Oh."

We are walking along South Bank arm in arm. Several barges make their way up the Thames, all carrying coal.

"I'd love to do that," he says. "Not on one of those, but a houseboat, journeying the canals. I read a book about it . . ."

"*Narrow Boat*!" I interrupt. "The book that started the whole Inland Waterway Association. Do you know Robert Aickman? He and Frankfort are very close friends. Story goes that he read the book, got in touch with its author, Tom Rolt, and the rest, they say, is history."

Russell looks at me, impressed.

"I've read his book of ghost stories, the one he wrote with Howard, can't remember her full name. There's a cracking tale in there called 'Three Miles Up' – it's the absolute stand-out tale in the whole collection. I bet you a pound it was he who wrote it!"

I do not correct Russell's mistake.

"We could hire a houseboat for a week or two and cruise 'the cut'," I say as Russell nods at a couple who pass us by. The lady's neck swivels as if on bearings.

"You could bring the typewriter, and . . ."

"What would you do?" Russell asks. He stops and stares at me intently.

"I'd read, I like to paint or maybe try and write something myself." I smile and stare at his crotch. "And do other things to pass the time."

RUSSELL - MEETING

"I'LL RETURN IN a couple, maybe three hours. Make good use of the television downstairs," I say to Emilia as I ready myself to leave the room. "If you do go out, leave me a note and I'll either come and find you or meet you downstairs for dinner."

"I love you," she says. I tell her I love her back.

I walk to the Reform Club, the place where Bertie is expecting me. The streets are busy, and even though the horse and cart is a dying breed, I am almost hit by one. My mind is not where it needs to be. The cart driver, an old man with one tooth in his mouth, spits at me, but misses.

"You dirty bast . . ." he screams amidst the sound of fast clip-clopping hooves.

I loosen my tie slightly, my throat is still tender from yesterday. This morning, before breakfast. I returned the favour. It feels dangerous, and something, if I had only discovered it or thought about it earlier, that could have brought Binky to life. I don't know, I think I'm kidding myself, not even Dr Frankenstein himself could have worked any miracles on frigid Binky.

Arriving at the Reform Club, I talk to a very elderly man on reception whose chest caves in when he breathes, much like that of a dying pigeon. I tell him who I am here to see. I must sign a big leather book with my name and my address and then I follow him, marvelling at the surrounding splendour.

"Mr van Thal, Mr Stickles," the Ancient says to Beritie, who is lost in a copy of *The Times*. He drop-folds the paper in on himself, smiles, those shark eyes again, then closes the paper and places it on the table which is already party to a large cut glass tumbler of scotch.

"Ah, Russell, how very good to see you!" Bertie says, genuinely, and shakes my hand. I am prepared this time and shake his back with equal vigour. He asks me to sit down on the leather wingback opposite his and ask me what I would like to drink.

"A Pussyfoot please. Still too early for me, I'm afraid."

"Not at all. You heard the gentleman," Bertie says to the elderly doorman.

"Yes, sir, of course."

"What do you think of the place, eh?" he beams. "I've been a member here for twenty years, and if you want to become a member of it, it's not a problem, I'll sponsor you in."

"It's very impressive," I reply, "but I'm not sure I'm in London enough to make use of it."

"Ah, that's where you've made a mistake, see? It's exactly for those times when you rarely come to the city, the place has Chambers so you can stay here overnight. You're a man of talent, this place is *made* for you."

He badgers me. He's not unlikeable, but he is a needler, will worry away at me like a dog at a bone. I must weigh this with the undeniable fact that this man will bring me income. Always be on the look-out to add feathers to your nest. But he'll want his 'cut'.

"I hear from Arnold that your book is their biggest selling since the war ended and it's only been out a few months. Congratulations!"

"Thank you, it's quite overwhelming, and of course work has already started on the second no..."

He interrupts me.

"I love the short story you sent, and I think it would be really good for your career to strike while the iron is hot. Yes, people will be expecting your second novel, but what about a collection of stories in the meantime? Weidenfeld and Nicolson, Gollancz, Arthur Barker, they're looking for a collection of short stories at the moment, any genre, take your fancy. I can act as your agent; I, of course, represent Robert Aickman's interests."

That name again.

"Aickman, ah yes, I would like to bend his ear somewhat about the canals."

"Would you like me to invite him here this morning? I have to say you look a little like him, but I suppose yours is not an uncommon face."

My Pussyfoot is brought to me and I drink it. The lemon juice makes my tongue zing. It is refreshing.

"Is he also based in London, or would he have to travel in?"

"He's in Gower Street, can be here in no time, if he's in. Just go easy on the canals, his zealotry knows no bounds. He'll try and get you signed up for his Inland Waterway nonsense; he tried it on with me but I told him that it wasn't to my taste, my feet like to be planted firmly on solid ground. You stay there, have a read of the paper and I'll go and give Robert a call, see if he's in."

I eat an egg and cress sandwich. It has been cut into little delicate triangles, crusts removed. They lie on a Reform Club paper napkin. I try to take a single, perfect bite, much like the Rector's child did, but I have a snaggletooth and the imprint it leaves on the sandwich upsets me. Bertie tucks into a steak on his return, juice drips from the tip of his knife.

"Mr van Thal, Mr Stickles – Mr Aickman," we are informed. I pat my mouth, rubbing away any errant egg crumbs with the napkin and stand up, smiling as I shake his hand. "A pleasure," I say.

We are not dissimilar, both wear heavy spectacles, however his lips are too feminine and he is younger than I, but only by a few years. His teeth are questionable to the point of unfixable.

Bertie just points to a spare chair.

"Sit down Bobbo, order a drink." he orders through a mouthful of food.

"You know I *despise* that name," Robert says, curtly. He picks up the menu and studies it languorously. The doorman has gone. A waiter, a young chap with an infuriatingly white pimple on his forehead hovers, waiting.

"No food, just a gin and tonic," he says, his voice clipped. He takes too long on both the 'a' and the 'n' in 'and', he elongates the word, loses the 'd' so it sounds more like 'aann'. A 'gin aann tonic'.

"So what book has Bertie signed you up for?" Aickman reaches for his drink. I look at the waiter, expecting he of the pimply forehead, but instead it's Binky, holding out a silver tray. She turns to me, holds her finger up to her lips. "Shh."

"Bertie's nibbling away at me. Waiter, can I have something a little stronger please?" I ask. Binky looks upset and she drifts away in a wisp of black smoke, leaving pimple to nod as I ask him for a double whisky.

I leave the Reform Club, unsteady on my feet, but with Robert's number to ring in the future, and a houseboat to take ownership of for a fortnight "or more, as long as you want, really, I'll inform Jeff to expect you," and a shaky promise from me after Aickman left, to van Thal, that I would give him a collection of short stories, probably ghost and horror ones.

"Good," says Bertie. "The market, on the horror side of things, will boom especially if a production company decides to bring out a couple of motion pictures that push at the edges of decency and add lashings of *grand guignol*, of this I am sure. People have put the war far behind them now, they need a bit of fright back in their lives."

I make sure that I will not be hit by any passing road user; car, animal or other and walk back to Claridges. I check in at reception to see if any messages have been left – I am expecting one from Frankfort – and I am right, he will be round to pick me up in the morning to take me to the Arnold offices.

Emilia is not there when I enter the room. She has left a note on the table by the window.

R, bored, have either nipped back to my flat or am doing the bookshops in Covent Garden. Will bring you back something meaty. E x

I make friends with the bed, one of the comfiest I have ever had the pleasure of lying on.

RUSSELL - CLUB

I WAKE UP, it is dark. I rub my eyes, unsure of my surroundings before it all floods back. I turn over, Emilia is sleeping, curled up. She must have snuck back in when she saw me asleep. I get up, walk to the en-suite, turn on the light and check my watch, 11pm. I pour myself a glass of water, having to let the tap run for a while. I feel muddled, but not hungover. I have been asleep since three, normally my nightly allowance. I sit on an austere-looking chair by the window and slightly open the net curtains, there are some signs of life out there. Now I am fully awake I decide that I want to walk. I scribble a note

E, Woke up, couldn't get back down, thought it churlish to wake you. Hopefully you haven't woken yourself and won't need to read this. R

At the reception I ask the night porter if it is okay to get a 'quick stiffener' and I follow him through to the bar where there is someone slumped in the corner. "One of our rich regulars. He makes a habit of it and we learned a long time ago never to wake him up. One of these days we'll nudge him and he won't respond."

I stare at the drunk's chest as he inhales and exhales. He is remarkably quiet; if it had been me I would be rattling out the odd roar of a snore.

The night porter hands me a glass of whisky, no ice. I down it, shuddering as the fire consumes me. I am left with a pleasing glow as it warms up my insides.

"Another?" he asks, taking my glass.

"When I return. I'm going to go for a bit of a walk, clear the head, cannot for the life of me get back to sleep."

"The door will be locked, always is at this time of night, just ring the bell and I'll let you back in," the night porter says as we leave the curved bar and the drunk behind to get on with his temporary oblivion.

I pull up the collar of my jacket and I stalk out into the night. I look up at the hotel behind me, making a guess as to which room is ours to see whether it has a light on or not. It does not.

I make short work of the streets, Binky is trying to keep up with me. It's funny, the little thing that happened in the Reform Club gave me more power over her than my little stunt back at the cottage did. My mother hasn't turned up for days now. I believe that it's just my mind and natural manifestation of guilt at losing my mother and covering up Binky's death. I simply couldn't have the village knowing that she had committed suicide. I would have had to have left, never to return and I like Effingham.

I am stopped by a policeman walking the beat. He asks me where I've come from and where I'm going. I tell him that I am staying at Claridge's, the look on his face makes it plain that he doesn't believe me.

"Phone them if you like."

"I will do; please, come with me."

We walk to a police box and he opens it up with his turnkey. I sigh as he places a call to Claridges. Binky fingers herself in front of us. Obviously the officer doesn't see this vulgar display.

"What's your name?"

"Stickles, Russell Stickles. Author." I throw the last piece in, just in case it makes him pause, but it does not. It is clear he is not a fan of reading.

After a few more minutes he hangs up, clearly disappointed. Binky pulls her hand away, one of her fingers is missing. She looks equally disappointed.

"Very sorry to have interrupted you, Sir, but you can't be too careful and I'm only doing my job."

"Well you've done it."

Before he can say anything further, I turn on my heel and walk away from him at an exceptionally quick pace. I entertain the thought of going straight back to the hotel, but that would mean that the jumped up little Stalin would win.

I cross the river at Westminster, barely bothering about Parliament, and make my way to a club that I have been a member of since the war. I didn't want to tell Bertie that I was a member of it. Not his business. I walk onto Kennington Road, turn off at Walcot Square and down St Mary's Walk. The club, the unnamed club, is hidden amongst the middle of St Mary's Gardens, cloaked by numerous Yew trees. The entrance to it is no more than a door in what appears to be a small tomb. I ring the intermains system and wait for the reply.

"Password?" a discombobulated voice asks. I cannot tell if it is male or female.

"'Foxtrot Oscar Papa." The password has changed recently to make use of the NATO phonetic language. I love it.

The door opens and swings outward. I walk down a thin set of stairs, down into a tunnel which curves slightly to the left before I enter a room where no smoking is allowed whatsoever; the air conditioning is minimal. There is a girl working tonight, unusual, they must have recently changed their policy. I order a Pussyfoot. If I start on the alcohol again the morning with Frankfort will be bruised. I find myself a leather wingback in the corner of the room and place my drink on the table and go look at the rows of books they have lining one of the walls. I pluck Chandler's *The Big Sleep,* one of the many I have always meant to read, but never got round to, and within moments am lost in his evocative and beautiful world.

The ringing of the intermains disturbs me. The girl at the bar presses down on a button and says "password."

"Room for Two" comes the reply, loud enough for me to hear. The girl looks down a list in front of her.

"Sorry, this is a year old, I cannot let you in. Please renew your membership through the usual channels."

"Fuck you, *cunt.*" I am taken aback by the language and I get up to offer my assistance but the girl holds her hand out and tells me that it won't be needed.

The buzzer is pressed again and whoever it is just will not stop. This makes a door at the side of the bar open. A small man comes out, slicked back bleach blonde hair and long arms, arms that simply seem too long for a man of his diminutive stature. Orangutan arms. He's no more than five foot three. He taps his forehead at the girl, she nods. He runs up the steps, the door opens, then a scream followed by a sickening series of thumps. The small man enters a moment later, dragging, with unusual strength, for he is a most unusual man, the annoyance who was trying to get in. He takes him through the bar, into the door he came out of. It closes behind him with a firm click.

"Of course, you saw nothing, Mr Stickles," the girl tells me, and I nod my head, remembering how I managed to get involved with a club such as this in the first place, but feeling very thrilled that I did.

She brings me a fresh Pussyfoot.

"On the house, for your troubles."

"Oh, no trouble at all," but I understand what she means. I drink the second Pussyfoot in two gulps and go to put the book back.

"Keep it, there's nothing worse than leaving a book half-read. Bring it back on your next trip. Please."

"Thank you," I say, tucking it into my coat. "I'll take good care of it."

"Thank you for stopping by. See you soon, Mr Stickles."

I return to the hotel, press the buzzer and thirty seconds or so later, the heavy door is opened. The night porter smiles at me and asks me if the policeman caused any further hassle.

"No, thank God. Absolute bloody jobsworth. He would have been the first to dob a fellow in for all sorts back in the war—"

"You served?" There is surprise in his voice. I don't call him out on it, it's a common misconception that many people have. I seem at odds with serving, that people don't think my body could function properly during the theatre of war.

"Yes. Most of this is tied up with the Official Secrets Act, but what I *can* say is that the noise of air rushing from a man's lung once you have shot him is one of the ugliest and terrifying noises I have ever heard." I leave it at that, as does he. I bid him a good morning as it is now three am. I was lost reading Chandler for more time than I realised. I make my way up the stairs and into the room.

Emilia is still asleep. I take the book out from my jacket, place it on the table and rip the note up. I get fully undressed and go to her, roll her over onto her back and tug off her knickers. She wakes, smiling.

We bump into Dennis Wheatley and his wife Joan at the foot of the stairs. We exchange pleasantries. I introduce them to Emilia then Dennis and I step to one side and say that it would be good to have a catch-up at some time and talk about the 'good old' days when we served together, with him as my superior at the London Controlling Section. He is completely unaware that I have a book published and is slightly taken aback that I am in Claridges in the first place.

We sit at our table and the waiter brings over a pot of coffee, and pours us both cups. It is scaldingly hot, and I temper it with a little milk and drop in one sugar. I am tired and anything to help pick up my energy is a boon. Emilia is talking to me about her family, and how she left them when she was seventeen to come and stay with an aunt in London. We are eating kippers in milk. The restaurant is quite quiet and for once Binky is nowhere to be seen.

"I've decided that I will rent a houseboat for a trip on one of the canals next month," I finish off a bite of fish. "I know we only alluded to it yesterday but *would* you like to come with me? I don't have the faintest idea of how we'll actually steer the thing, we'll have to take lessons on how to drive it, I'm sure!"

EMILIA - HIDDEN

I AM IN my room surrounded by clothes. I am having difficulty picking out the most suitable items; the BBC informs that the weather for the next week will be changeable, so I don't want to only pack heavy items such as cardigans or woollen skirts. I look at the copy of *An Uneasy Dream* I was given by Frankfort. I pick it up and leaf through it, the margins are crammed with notes, I have underlined many, many lines. I don't ever want Russell to see this copy. I put the book on the bed and go to my dresser, clear it of items then lift the dresser off the rug. I pull the rug back, revealing one floorboard that has a small notch in it. I use the end of a fork to prise it up and once free go back to *Dream* and put it in the roomy space along with my advanced copy of Thomas Caine's *Once Found, Always Found.* Thomas. I smile as I think about him, he had a beautiful soul. I take out *Once Found* and open it up, and stare at the newspaper cutting I placed in it.

BUDDING AUTHOR DIES
IN MYSTERIOUS CIRCUMSTANCES

I close the book, put it back in the floorspace, and gently touch the unknown and unpublished manuscript of Thomas' second work, *Thrown Away One Thoughtless Day.*

Russell meets me outside Liverpool Street and helps me with my suitcase when the Hackney pulls up. I pay the driver and then kiss Russell and mini-jump with excitement.

"It's so lovely of you to come down and meet me," I say to him when we are sitting in the carriage. There is a young boy, about six or seven sticking his tongue out at us. His mother is reading a book and is doing her best to ignore his rudeness.

"Well, it's certainly diverting me from having to pack – the weatherman says one thing, then another and it's sending me into a right state!"

I laugh and explain my own woes. I've put in a couple of summer frocks, a bathing suit, but also a thick jumper and a pair of slacks, I hope you don't mind?"

"Mind? Why would I mind? What an odd thing to say."

He stares at me, my cheeks burn. "I just want to be feminine for you, darling," I breathe, snuggling into his neck.

The woman reading her book gives out a cluck of exasperation; I do not know if this is because of what she is reading or what I have said.

At Clemendy I put the kettle on the stove and make sandwiches for lunch. Russell is out in the garden, an overgrown affair of swaying grasses and yet to fruit blackberry bushes. He's sat at a heavily weathered table, making notes, chewing on the end of his pencil in thought before bending down to write again. I take the cheese from the larder and cut liberal slices and place them on the slices of buttered bread. As I cut through the sandwiches I smell burning, coming from within the cottage. I put down the knife and do a quick tour. There is no fire and I am unsure as to where the smell is coming from. Probably a farmer burning the stubble in one of his fields, I mull, as I re-enter the kitchen.

I look out at Russell, he is still oblivious to the world around him. I rub my forehead, the cluster of a headache starting to make itself known. I gather together a few tomatoes, cut them in half, sprinkle them with salt and sit with Russell outside and we eat in silence.

I am in bed, my headache has blossomed into something truly terrible. They've been nagging me for a couple of weeks now, on and off. Russell walked into town to the pharmacy and came back with pain relief that is still to take hold. He is sitting by the bed, the lamp on the floor by his feet, it throws up a soothing light. He is reading to me a section from his latest short story.

Starr walked through the graveyard when out of the corner of his eye he spotted a gentleman wearing a baby blue blazer, slacks and shoes. It was a colour he had never seen an adult wear, it was a shade more befitting a newborn boy. He wanted to walk to him, to see what he was up to, but that would have been rude, 'unbecoming' as his wife liked to say at any given opportunity. Starr inwardly shrugged the thought of the man away and walked up the path and into the church, sitting down on the hard bench. He was there for about five minutes when a woman came in and sat directly in front of him. She was all in pastel pink, from the hat on her head to her jacket skirt, and yes, shoes. Starr looked at her legs. She was not wearing tights. Starr immediately got up, the oddness of it all becoming much too much and he left the church, where he physically bumped into the man in baby blue in the porch. It was almost as if the man had been waiting for him to leave.

"I like it," I say, "but I'm really losing concentration, can you read the rest of it tomorrow when we're on the houseboat?"

Russell's rector friend comes and picks us up in his car and drives us to the train station with our luggage. They shake hands and the Rector drives off, the exhaust in his car chugging out such a plume of thick black smoke that it makes both of us cough and unable to breathe for thirty seconds or so until the smoke clears.

"I hope the bloody car conks out on him," Russell says, coughing again.

The houseboat is called *Phosphorus* and has been hired from Jeff Thomson at Rickmansworth. It is boat No. 66, reg. R.A. 26281, tastefully painted. Many of the narrowboats around us are garish. I ask about the boats surrounding us in the harbour, if they ever see action on 'the cut'.

"Tha' dinnae move, 'less it's time tae dry dock 'em" the harbour master says, his Scottish accent so thick as to be almost impenetrable.

"A hard life?" Russell asks, genuinely interested.

RUSSELL - SLOW

MAN, WOMAN AND child are all looking at us when we get on the houseboat, or the slowboat as Jeff calls it, after we have loaded all of our food, luggage and alcohol on. The place looks snug, and while there will be a slight adjustment time, I don't see any real issue. If the worst comes to the worst I can sleep on the roof with a few blankets, there are rails that run down either side of the roof, so I won't roll off.

Jeff is a patient teacher, and when we leave the jetty on which we are moored, having first been told how to tie knots correctly, I do not let on that in my previous life knots were a foregone conclusion. He also teaches us how the engine works (again, I remain silent) and we are informed that there will be several stops on our journey where we can refill the boat with fuel.

"The barge doesn't go over four miles an hour, and remember when you are travelling the canal, if there are others moored, go past them at two miles an hour, the noise and the wake that your boat will create can make theirs bob about unnecessarily."

We are keen students, with both of us having a go at steering the longboat. There are no locks on this particular stretch of canal, but in thirty miles there will be several. The volunteer lock-keepers will help us with that, and we will soak up everything that they do. Once Jeff is happy with us we are off, slowly putt-putting away from pairs of small urchin eyes who stare at us intently as we begin our journey.

I have taken off my shirt and am in my vest, the sun is out and doesn't seem to want to go back in until evening.

"This is *perfect*," Emilia sighs, snuggling up next to me, her arm draped round my waist. I smile, but am completely concentrating on driving the houseboat. As slowly as this thing may move I am more than aware that there will be patches of the trip where parts won't be as clear of detritus and we might get stuck.

"Why don't you go and make us a nice cup of tea? Or if you want me to go and start the wood burner, can you take over?"

"Please, if you can start the burner, that would be lovely, thank you."

I duck into our living quarters and scrunch up the sports section of the day's newspaper, something I will never read, and throw it into the wood burner, then place strips of kindling, kindly supplied to us by Jeff. The fire takes hold quickly, and I throw the curled charcoal match into the flames. I then put several split logs into the burner, close the door and open the vent, giving it enough oxygen to really take hold. I can hear Emilia sing through the noise of the engine. It sounds like a swarm of content bees. I fill up the small metal kettle from one of several glass jars of water and put it on the stove part of the burner and stay with it until it boils. I make the tea, sweet, as we both prefer it, three sugars in each.

"Here you go, " I say, climbing up the steps to where she stands, resting against the back bar. She looks almost ethereal with the sun behind her.

She takes the cup from me and places it on the roof. I sit on one of the deck chairs, also supplied, and take a sip on the tea, taking in my surroundings as we slowly glide through the day. A family of ducks swim alongside us.

The afternoon passes by pleasingly, Emilia makes lunch, thick ham sandwiches slathered with fine, grainy mustard. We are trying to make it as far as The Squirming Grub, a hostelry on the edge of the river near the village of Bondham. There is a 15th century chapel I would like to visit. It contains the tomb of 'Peter the Strangler', a vicar who served his parish, by all accounts with passion and dedication, but who after his death in 1799, was accused of several murders, previously attributed to a simpleton who helped out at the church called Chumly Drury. These claims were all denied by the Church of England, of course, until a diary was found behind a panel in the eaves of the church after it was damaged by a stray bomb in early 1941. The diary was in Peter Recorderant's own hand and pretty much confirmed what had always been suspected but denied. The Church apologised for Recorderant's misdeeds and made restitution by paying compensation of £100 to each of the families descendants, all of whom still live in the village. They wouldn't move the tomb, their thinking behind it being that more people would come to the church to visit and they were right. If I remember rightly, the book was published by the person who found it, a volunteer fireman who in 'real life' was a local historian. The Church had made angry protestations, threatening to sue if it was published, but Recorderant was long out of copyright, had no kin and the Church just buried their head in the sand when the book was brought out to great controversy, but visitor numbers were higher than ever before and the contribution boxes were always full.

I take over from Emilia and she goes to lie down for a little while, the heat is indeed punishing. I had let the fire die down in the living-quarters, as soon as our cups of tea were made. The space, even with windows fully-open, is turning into an oven. There are going to be quite a few mistakes made until we get this longboating down to a fine art, I feel.

I see a boat moored up to the left of me, so I cut the throttle down and we idle by at two miles per hour. There is an elderly man sitting on the roof of his vessel. He is naked from the waist up and has a snow white beard that reaches his belly button. However there is a circle of brown and yellow around his mouth, the effects of his cigarette smoking. I smile briefly then look away, it isn't a pleasing sight and makes me feel slightly angry that you would choose to live your life looking as if you permanently had your mouth affixed to someone's anus.

I turn the throttle up halfway past his vessel, the sudden surge in power sends out a swell that rocks the elderly man's boat. I presume that it knocks him overboard, as I hear a splash as I continue on. I do not look back.

Three miles further down the 'cut' we come to a split in the canal. I make my way down the right hand side, steering carefully, revving and slowing, revving and slowing until I am fully in the new canal. There is a sea of bulrushes, also known as reed mace, correct latin name *Typhaceae*, to the right of me. I look at these warily, to crash into them would be chaotic, and bring our journey to a premature end.

Emilia joins me an hour or so later, wearing nothing but my white shirt and smoking a cigarette. She sits on the roof of the boat and slowly parts her legs. I let my hand wander. She takes a last deep drag of her smoke before she flicks the unfiltered remains into the canal and leans back on both of her hands for support. She orgasms heavily, my fingers shine with her juice. I make a great show of licking them, much to her delight. She returns the favour with her mouth, the only witnesses to our carnal acts are indifferent horses and cattle in the fields on either side of the canal.

I check that the mooring is tied and the longboat will not drift off during our trip to The Squirming Grub. We walk, hand in hand, down a path that cuts through a waist-height thicket and there it is, an eighteen-century building with a suitable pleasing thatched roof that looks as if it has been recently replaced.

We enter, the place is busy and we find a table under the window. The only food they have on offer is a homemade pie, which suits us both and I go and get us two pints of bitter. The landlord is kind and chats amiably enough, showing me his collection of emperor penguin ornaments on a shelf behind him.

The pie has a thick crust, unctuous gravy and tender chunks of beef and kidney. It's exactly what we need and we demolish our meals in minutes, both resting back against our chairs, groaning.

I wake, slightly hungover. Emilia is already up, stoking the fire and making a cup of much needed tea. The bed, a small double, that we ourselves had to assemble, was surprisingly comfortable. And although I found it difficult to sleep, Emilia curling up tight against me was an adequate consolation prize.

Binky is sitting on the roof of the longboat as we sit in our deck chairs on the towpath. We are ready to move if we spy a horse. They are regularly used to tow some of the longer coal barges. There is plenty of excrement on the path as proof.

Emilia sniffs the air experimentally, then rubs her temples briefly, her eyes squinting. Binky notices this and slides down from the roof with no guide rails and onto the path next to Emilia.

"She knows I'm here!" says Binky, wonder and excitement in her cracked, burnt voice.

I say nothing for fear of alarming Emilia, and I will not be cowed by my own mind's cruel games. I throw the remains of my tea into the water and snap close my deck chair and say that we should be getting a move on and walk into Bondham. Binky hisses at me and drifts off, ash taken by a sudden wind.

The walk is pleasant. We are on a road with high hedgerows, almost like the kind you would find in Devon or Cornwall. Emilia is holding my hand, Binky grasping firmly onto the other, trying to tug me away, big flakes of burnt skin falling onto the floor and revealing her cooked flesh. Try as I might, this time I just can't get her to leave.

We make our way into Bondham. The hedgerows ease as we approach the outskirts of the village which has a line of big Elm trees lining the road, their branches intertwining, creating a canopy where sunshine dapples through. Children are playing in their front gardens, on the street and I half expect one to point at us and see Binky and start screaming.

We stop by a newsagent and I buy a packet of Spangles for Emilia and a Toff-o-Luxe for myself. Binky vanishes again. I really need to make an appointment to see a doctor. It's now becoming an itch I have no wish to scratch. I ask for directions to the church and am told that it is on the other end of the village, up a hill called Grave's End.

"Half an hour or less?" I ask.

"Nowhere near that, fifteen at a stretch. The village isn't that big, but the hill, it's a killer and why it's called Grave's End, you need to rest in one after you reach the place!"

I laugh, this exchange tickles me.

We walk up the hill and it is punishing, I start to wheeze halfway up the hill. Emilia laughs and calls me an old man and starts to push me. This is the first time Emilia has ever mentioned our age difference. I am 44, she is 26, but I like to think I look younger. Indeed Binky, when she was alive always said I looked 'youthful'. I do not want to ask her what I look like to her today.

The church is as expected, but bigger than I thought it would be. The tomb of Peter the Strangler has remarkably been left alone, I had thought it a certainty that someone would have vandalised it by trying to rub Peter's name out or scratching it away with a knife or some other sharp implement. As loath as I am to leave money to the church, Emilia persuades me to put a shilling in the collection box.

On our way back to the longboat we pick up supplies from the village shop which sits next door to a large primary school. Interestingly it has a *memento mori* carved high under one of the roof arches and I mentally make a note to ask someone about it before we leave the area. We buy bread, cheese, a pint of milk and several bottles of beer and we cheerfully split the weight between us as we walk out of the village.

"What was your wife like?" Emilia asks. We are sitting on the path by the boat, watching the sun slowly sink.

I decide on whether to shut down, but I would rather her not be in a foul mood because of something I have done or not done.

"She was two years younger than I. We met when I left the service. We courted for a month or so before she moved in. Mother liked her at first, in fact they got along very well, but then a couple of years ago when mother got sick things became very bad between them and I was stuck in the middle. I was piggy."

When Emilia is fast asleep I get up off the bed - luckily it does not creak – and I quickly get dressed. I put on a dark jumper. It's thin so I do not think I'll become too hot in it.

I make my way to the church, pausing for breath again up Grave's End. It feels good though, walking along in the middle of the night, whatever light of the moon there is guiding the way.

I have taped a patch of black cloth to my torch and have cut a small hole in the middle of it. I turn on the torch when I reach the church porch. Putting the light in my mouth to hold it steady, I carefully lift up the heavy iron handle and turn it with both hands, my movements slow and sure. The door does not creak as I push it inwards.

My footsteps are soft, the thin beam of light taking me to my destination. I walk twelve steps, stop, turn ninety degrees to the right, walk another five steps and put my hand on the money box. I use a penknife to make short work of the flimsy lock. The box is heavy when I pick it up. There is no getting round making a noise while pouring the money into the cotton bag I have brought with me.

I walk away from the church at a brisk pace, the torch tucked into the back of my trousers, the cotton bag the coins are in is folded over and tied tightly with string to minimise the noise it could make. I do not risk taking the bag onto the boat, so I hide it as the hedgerow starts again, dislodging a stone, putting the bag in there and replacing the stone. I step back, it doesn't look out of place at all and I could easily find it when I next return.

I creep back onto the boat. Emilia is still asleep. I take the covering off the torch and throw it into the log burner and cover it with ash. I light a candle and read, my latest book is Gabriel García Márquez's *La Hojarasca* published in its native Spanish. I hope it will be translated one day. Although I understand most of it, I feel that I'm losing quite a lot of the subtext, but it is still enjoyable. Márquez's technique is interesting by starting the book, to quote the Latin, *in medias res*, in the middle of things. There are multiple narrators, internal monologues, streams of consciousness throughout and it makes for an altogether heady mix. He is also a proponent of a term that I heard discussed for the first time this year. I *think* it is an apt description of his work - 'magic realism' – the portrayal of the 'magical' nature and order of the rational world.

I want to wake up Emilia and tell her about the book, it enthuses me greatly, but then I realise that I am still full of adrenalin from my late night church visit. I unfold the deckchair and sit on the towpath and look up at the millions of stars.

EMILIA - FALL

THE STARTING OF the engine wakes me up. I yawn and stretch like a cat on the bed, then get up and pad my way to Russell.

"Morning," I say, yawning and kissing him on the cheek. He smiles briefly and points at the sky.

"Look at how beautiful it is already, but it's going to be another scorcher and we need to get a move on and find a good place to find shade before it gets too hot."

"What time is it?"

"Seven. Early, but not obscene."

I go back and get my packet of Kensitas and light one, filling the cabin with smoke. For an instant, a brief instant, I can see a woman's face in amongst the swirling greyness, but I put this down to just waking up.

"Cup of tea?" I shout through the din of the engine.

"Yes please. Want me to start the fire?"

"No, I'll be able to manage it, darling."

Russell is continuously on the tiller so we make good time. We pass a farmer on his tractor, Russell slows down to a stop and we chat to him about his work and if the land is his or belongs to someone else.

"Excuse me?" a voice from behind us says. A policeman cycles up to the narrowboat. Russell nods goodbye to the farmer who seems loathe to leave, but starts up his machine and drives away.

"Officer!" he says, stepping onto the path. "How can I help you?" Russell smiles and grabs the man by the hand, shaking it hard. The policeman seems instantly disarmed.

"Oh, very well thanks . . . what are your names please?"

We both tell him.

"Just a question, did you pay a visit to the church in Bondham yesterday?"

"Of course," Russell says. "We went early, got directions from the newsagent, he wasn't wrong about how steep the hill was, and we spent, what, about half an hour there?" Russell looks in my direction. I also step off the boat onto the path, but carry the mooring rope which I lash around a stone post that has been cemented into the ground.

I am wearing one of Russell's shirts again but with knickers on this time. The policeman looks embarrassed and can barely look my way.

"What's the matter, officer?" I ask.

This question perks him up.

"Well, the sad fact is that a collection box in the church was broken into and the contents robbed."

"Oh no," we both say at the same time. "How awful," I continue. "We even put a shilling in it yesterday. How much was taken?"

"A sizeable amount, ten pounds. The vicar had been meaning to empty it that day, but had been waylaid as one of his parishioners had died in the early evening. When he went round first thing this morning it had gone. I was called and both the newsagent and grocery shop owner mentioned you. I came down to the mooring but you had gone."

"Officer . . . Officer?"

"Officer Monroe."

"Ah, Officer Monroe, of course, I can see why you want to talk to us, but rest assured, we don't have the money, it wasn't us," Russell says, quite calmly. "You are more than free to check the boat, but if it's too much for you to handle, you can call any other police officer down as well to search. The only reason we moved this morning," Russell says, pointing at the sun, "is that thing in the sky. Where we were we would have baked like an oven and we just wanted to find a cool spot for the rest of the day, which, I believe, is not too far away, the next mooring is next to a pub . . . I believe it to be called The Potted Plant?"

"You're right."

"So, I have an idea, bring your bike, put it on the roof and we'll make our way to there. We'll then close up the boat and walk with you to the pub, you can place your phone call and get in touch with your colleagues. We'll be with you at all times."

"If you're sure sir, you certainly are going out of your way for me."

"Yes, it *is* an inconvenience for us, but nothing compared to the loss that the church has suffered. We know our consciences are clear and are not guilty but you don't. This way we can get this over and done with and continue on with our holiday. Agreed?"

"Agreed," the policeman mirrors. Russell looks at me and shrugs, *what else can we do*? I'm impressed with his handling of the officer, he's clearly had experience in dealing with this type of official before. His past is an undiscovered country. No traveller returns, puzzles the will.

Russell takes the officer's bike and puts it on the roof. I unhitch the rope from the mooring and invite the officer on. He goes into the boat's

65

bowels. Russell asks me to take us to the pub. Once the engine is started I take hold of the tiller and guide the way to the pub, about a mile away. Once there we all make our way up, the policeman having to knock on the door. He asks to be let in to make a call.

"I was really hoping to get a spot of writing done today," Russell sighs once a contingency of officers had left and were all in agreement that no illicit money was on board.

"So, what did you do with the money? Where did you hide it? I heard you leave the boat last night," I question, instantly furious with myself.

Russell smiles ever so gently.

"Yes, I did leave the boat, but I didn't go up to the church. Found a tree stump to sit on and watched the sky for an hour or so. I find your accusation disappointing. This is your first mistake in my company. I pray that it will be your last. The pub is going to open shortly, shall we see if we can get a spot to eat? I'm famished."

He leaves me, his cutting dismissal makes my face burn with embarrassment.

"My, that's one of the best meals I've had in a long time, and I try to stay clear of fish," Russell remarks, mopping up sauce from the plate with a slice of bread. "The night my mother died, I had food poisoning. Fish pie. Nothing as fresh as this." He leans back in his chair, smiling with satisfaction. I have barely touched my food. He does not, or does not *want* to, notice my plate.

"I'd like to stay here tomorrow and move on the day after, if that's alright with you." He reaches and touches my hand. "I would like to try and get a little bit of writing done, and this place certainly can cook up a good meal, we would be foolish to leave in a hurry. Besides," and here he winks at me, "I'm sure that Officer Monroe and the local constabulary will be following our every move."

I clear away the leftovers from breakfast and tell Russell that I'm going to go for a walk. He barely registers my existence, his fingers are hammering away at his typewriter, his body the conduit, tapped into some mysterious source of which even he doesn't know the location. I slip on my shoes and pull a jumper over my blouse. Unlike the previous day, it's overcast. I walk past the pub in the direction of the next village on the map, Hussnam. I sing softly to myself, playing over in my mind our 'confrontation'. Was it really though? Did he think I simply had 'a moment' was stupid enough to blurt it out and came down hard on me *just* enough to quell any doubts that I might have about him. That in its own way hid my mistake from him, that I was of a mind that didn't think along linear lines. Damn.

I am so lost in my own thoughts that I don't hear the car until the last second, look up and twist my body out of the way, as if by magic, land in a heap. The car screeches to a halt. Two men get out, the passenger, dressed in mushroom-coloured slacks and a beautifully tailored suit makes his way towards me. He is wearing thick-rimmed glasses, and for a second I think it is Russell, there is a vague similarity to their faces. The gentleman has one hand clutched in the other. It is on fire. I stare in horror as flames race over his face, going into his mouth and down his throat. I try to scream, but a massive, punishing bolt bursts in my head.

RUSSELL - GONE

MY STOMACH RUMBLES. I look at my watch. It has just gone one. Emilia has not returned for lunch. Sighing, I make myself a cucumber sandwich and open up one of the last bottles of beer. I go out into the light and sit by the canal, my legs swinging, milimetres from touching the water. I demolish the sandwich in a few bites, but take my time with the beer. I am pleased with how my writing has gone, I have finished a new story. I don't know what I'm going to call it yet, but it has a character in it called Emilia. That should hopefully appease her. I do feel bad about how I treated her, but never in a million years was I going to admit to doing that. As odd as the air is around her, I don't think she's criminally swayed. It would just cause too much trouble.

It is five o'clock and she still hasn't returned. I worry that she's left me, not caring about her belongings. The tone I took with her was too firm. I walk up to The Potted Plant and go in. A familiar face, a London face, sitting at a table with a friend.

"Aickman? Robert Aickman?" I ask.

Aickman looks up and smiles when he sees me.

"My days, Russell, how great it is to see you, and not under Bertie van Thal's corpulent shadow! Please, come over and meet my friend, this is Sebastian Carruthers, one of the IWA members. We were in the area looking at a stretch of canal a couple of miles from here that we want to do some pretty immediate work on. Drink?"

"Yes please. By any chance you've not seen a girl on your travels? Pretty thing with curly brown hair, wearing red lipstick? I can't find her, I'm going out of my mind, I'm just about to call the police."

Aickman's face falls.

"Ah, yes, we did see a girl fitting that description earlier today. In fact, Carruthers here nearly knocked her over. She banged her head pretty badly and we rushed her to the hospital. She's with you? Right, we'll drive you there. I say we, I don't drive. Sebastian does all of that."

"Thank you." I try to steady my breathing, the surreal nature of it all threatening to overwhelm me. "We were up here on the cut, as per your advice. Leased a boat from Jeff Thomson, as you suggested," I say as we leave the pub and walk towards the car.

"Which one?"

"The *Phosphorus*."

"A good little vessel. I've been on her before. Had any trouble with her?"

"None."

Aickman calms me down on the journey to the hospital, tells me about the canal they are trying to get money for. I nod, but it all goes over my head. He notices that I am still not fully at ease and assures me that she will be fine.

"She's being looked after, the hospital isn't that far away. Another seven miles or so."

I rush into the hospital, leaving Aickman and Sebastian in the car. They say they'll wait for me, which is incredibly kind. I am stopped by the Matron. I think she looks upon the fact that we are unmarried with some distaste, but she leads me to where Emilia is lying in bed.

"You have ten minutes."

Her face is pale, waxy, non-committal. I sit on the hard, upright chair that's next to her bed and hold her hand. She does not seem aware of my presence at first, then she slowly comes to life, like a reel of film passing through the light of a projection bulb.

"It's me, Russell," I say. "Do you know who I am?"

She smiles and tells me that I'm burning and that I really need to pat myself out before I do myself damage.

"Emilia, what's happened?"

"The burnt woman, she's setting fire to *everything*," she whispers, her eyes darting around the room. "She's set fire to you too, can't you see that?"

My heart quickens in my chest. Fear tickles my spine.

Emilia closes her eyes and drifts off.

"She's been like that since she came in. We're waiting for the nod from the hospital in Martown to take her – they have an X-Ray machine, we don't have that luxury," the Matron says behind me. I get up and turn to her, aghast.

"Something catastrophic has happened to her. Did she bang her head? The man who brought her in said they didn't hit her, but that she fell back."

"The doctor that examined her can't be sure, but he thinks that she may have a tumour, hence the hallucinations she's having."

"Do you have a telephone I can use? I'll pay."

"Follow me." She takes me to a bare room away from the main ward.

I place a call to Frankfort.

"Frankfort, it's Emilia, she's in a bad way. In hospital. Do you have her address? She's going to be here for a while, and I'll need to go and collect some things for her, she didn't bring enough with her."

"I didn't know that you two were together."

"It's not something that we've been hiding. She's been really good company when I've been writing."

Frankfort gives me her address and hangs up. I get the location of the new hospital from the Matron. I tell Emilia that I'll see her in a day. Her eyelids flicker as I lean over and kiss her on the forehead.

Aickman drops me off at the train station.

"Don't worry about the longboat. I'll be in the area for the next couple of days, I'll make sure that it's not bothered."

"Thank you very much for this," I say, shaking his hand hard.

"It's all very odd. It's like something in her head has just *popped*," Aickman sighs, flicking away a strand of hair that falls onto his face.

The carriage is empty and, for this I am thankful. It is hot and I wish to take off my blazer. If I was on the canal with Emilia this would not be a problem. But in here, if anyone was to come in I would be looked at with disdain, I'm sure.

I close my eyes and think of the War. I think of the mission Wheatley sent me on, to flush out the traitor who was working at one of our biggest newspapers. The look of surprise, then horror, when I spoke to him in fluent German telling him that the game was up. How I told him to be quiet as he started crying when he saw me take the cord out from my pocket. He lunged at me of course, that made it easier to place the hoop around his neck and pull. I dragged him, kicking to the door handle and tied the cord tight. How I crouched in front of him, our noses almost touching, his frothing spittle covering my face. The colour his face went, deeper than purple, darker than blue. How I breathed in *his* last breath. The . . .

"Next stop Liverpool Street," the ticket inspector says.

"Ha! Must have drifted off, thank you for that."

I am in Emilia's room. It takes me ten seconds to scan my surroundings and the way the dresser is angled on the rug, one leg too close to the edge, makes me smile. A policeman would never have been able to decode this. I am not a policeman.

I lift up the floorboard with a butter knife and I am now the possessor of Emilia's many secrets. She dances with darkness. And she is dancing with me.

I know what Emilia's game is, and she was waiting to collect. She has been waiting to collect until her brain decided otherwise. I look at the advanced copy of my book. Every page is scribbled with notes. There are too many to read, but she has appeared to get a lot out of the book. I look at the advance copy of Thomas Caine's *Once Found, Always Found*. I open it up and a slip of newspaper falls to the floor. I pick it up and I chuckle. My darling darkling. She has also made the most she can from Thomas' book. I wonder if he pleasured her on a canal boat.

I pick up a bound sheaf of papers, a manuscript called *Thrown Away One Thoughtless Day*. I put everything into my satchel. I put the floorboard, rug and dresser back into their correct place. I search through the rest of her room methodically, I find a gold necklace. I put it in my pocket. I put several items of Emilia's clothing in a net bag and leave her lonely world behind. A picture of Rita Hayworth in a lace-flower dress appeals with lust-filled eyes for me to stay.

"I told you she was bad news," Binky says as I walk down the stairs and out of the building.

RUSSELL - CONTINUE

I TAKE THE train to the new hospital to drop off Emilia's clothing. I am asked if I would like to pay her a visit but I tell the Sister that I am in a rush, I have to get back home. I jump back on the train and travel for two stops down another line and make my way back to the *Phosphorous*. It is as I left it. I open up and once the door is closed behind me, I lie on the unmade bed. It smells of us.

Emilia's intentions are not honourable. This makes me sad. I of course knew that there was *some* game afoot, but never did I realise that it would end up with her collecting my current manuscript and my fate determined by whatever accident I happened to find myself in.

I take a bottle of scotch from the cupboard in the kitchen area and pour a large glass. I drink and drink, not minding the fire until the liquor is gone.

I then sit at the typewriter and roll fresh pieces of paper and carbon in.

LOOSENING
Russell Stickles

Penelope didn't do love, she thought it obscene in the way that normal people find peep shows or dirty magazines obscene. What she did do, and did well, was pretend that she could love, should be loved, could be in love. She lied to herself and to the world around her. It was a mask that she was easily able to slip on and off as and when the fancy took her. Hearts were there to break and that she did, countless times to countless men.

It is dawn. I look at the pile of paper beside me and the stubs of candles. My eyes are heavy. My collection is finished. I get up, a pang of pain kicks in at my lower back. I stop, roll one more sheet of paper in and type.

This book is dedicated to Emilia Goldstone. Collector of pieces.

I separate all the sheets from the carbon and then tie-up the manuscripts with heavy twine. The finished book is about twenty-five thousand words long, exactly what Bertie asked for. I put everything in the satchel, it's heavy. I put my jacket over it.

EMILIA - DRIVE

I SIT IN silence in the back of the car. The woman did not want me picked up, this I can tell. The driver is chatty and I nod and smile and answer his questions. I tell them that I am on holiday with my husband. I am not telling them complete falsehoods. I feel queasy and I ask the driver to pull up a mile away from the longboat. I walk carefully, they did not notice I was not wearing shoes. The smell of the surrounding countryside soothes me. The noise of the wind through the trees distracts me a little from the burnt woman who walks beside me, telling me the best way to relieve Russell of the grief he is living with.

I arrive on the path which is much easier to walk on and step over a mound of fresh horse manure. My hands are in the pockets of a jacket I stole. I see the canal boat in front of me. I can hear Russell whistling. It's a pleasing tune, not one I've heard before. I stop and let his noise please me before it is snatched by the wind and carried off.

RUSSELL - END

I MAKE A sandwich. There is a knock on the hatch.

"Come in!" I shout, expecting Aickman.

"Hello darling," Emilia says. She looks like a ghost. She is wearing a baggy jacket, a man's. Worse than a ghost. She uneasily steps down into the hold.

I grab her and lead her in, sit her down.

"How did you get here, did you escape?"

"I wasn't in an *asylum*, Russell. I simply walked out."

"Are you feeling better?"

"The doctors say that it's brain cancer. My brain is slowly being eaten away. They want me to stay, of course they do. But we have a holiday to finish. And you have your book to finish. Then we'll see. Can we have a change of scene? Can you take us up to the next place? There was a pub you mentioned, The Still Moon. I'd like to visit it, please."

I take a bite out of my sandwich, looking at her. She doesn't need to know. She'll slip away soon. Why not make this as pleasant as possible for her? I chew, swallow.

"Okay, would you like me to take your jacket?"

"No." She pulls it in tight around her.

I start the engine and we chug our way along the canal. The wind blows slightly, carrying with it the smell of incoming rain.

She stands next to me, grabbing onto the rail for support.

"Ahead. What's that?"

I check the map.

"The Drake Tunnel. Two miles long. Hope that no-one comes along the other way. It's going to need someone to steer and someone at the front of the boat with a torch. What would you like to do?" I ask her.

"I'll sit in the front." Do you have a lighter?" She pulls out a crumpled packet of cigarettes from her pocket, a brand that she never smokes, Virginia Reds. I give her the tiller and duck into the hold and retrieve the Zippo from the box of candles. I pass it over and our fingers touch. It's like touching a plucked chicken.

I slow the boat to a halt as she clambers onto the roof to the other end of the boat with one of the deckchairs and the torch. It is easier than her climbing out of the front hatch. Once she is sitting comfortably, she looks at me and says quietly, "We need the burning woman to show us the way."

I smile and say that the torch will supply ample light. I make my way to the back of the boat, rev up the engine and make our way towards the mouth of the tunnel. It envelopes us, gobbles us up. The orange torch light in the front of our longboat is but a speck.

"Are you okay?" I yell.

"Yes, it's raining in here. How can it be raining?"

"It's just the water condensation coming off the ceiling." The first splashes hit my face, one drop rolling into my mouth. It tastes foul and I grimace.

"I love you, Russell," Emilia yells.

"I love you too," I lie.

"We're going to be very happy together," she shouts, "very happy." She then falls silent and we chug along.

I look behind me and the entrance is now a tiny white speck in the distance. I cannot see the space in front of me, I cannot see the walls of the tunnel although I can feel them around me. I cough, and cough again, taken by surprise at the smoke which surrounds me.

"Emilia?" I choke, shielding my mouth, trying to see through the darkness. A dancing flame. A dancing fire.

Emilia is on fire. She is crackling.

Emilia is screaming. I make my way into the hold, it is also filling with smoke. I can see Emilia through the crack in the blistering doors. She is sitting on the chair, also a-flame. She is being consumed. Binky is sitting with her holding her hand. I am taken back to that long ago night in the Anderson shelter. I cough, find my satchel and get out of the hold. I push the throttle down as far as it will go and jump off the longboat, into the choppy water which comes up to my neck. I hold my satchel up over my head and walk back, feet slipping on the floor of the canal and towards the small speck of daylight.

I throw my satchel up on the grass. I try and pull myself up, but my head dips under the water. This isn't so bad. This isn't. This is. This.

Arms grab me, I am dragged up. Dirty work faces stare at me. I retch, bringing up canal water.

"My friend is in there. She set fire to herself."

We wait at the exit to the tunnel. My clothes are heavy, my breathing horrendous. I cough and cough, bringing up more of the canal mixed with black phlegm.

Smoke comes in a dirty black wave out from the tunnel. It billows up into cloudy sky. An "Oooh!" goes up.

The longboat limps out. The front is completely destroyed. The back of it is starting to catch, The engine is turning, but slowly, wanting to die. The roof of the longboat has collapsed, but this has not stopped Binky and Emilia from dancing in amongst the ruins. My mother appears by my side and cuddles me.

"She's a nice addition to the family. We'll leave you be now, my love. We can manage from here."

Binky and Emilia stop dancing.

They both look at me sadly.

Seconds later they are both completely consumed by smoke.

Mother is no more.

As the boat drifts past us all I am left with are many questions from those gathered around me.

I am in the Reform Club. Frankfort, Robert and Bertie are listening to the last day of Emilia Goldstone. All are aghast.

"She had a tin of lighter fluid fused to her hand." I say. "The police are happy that it's suicide."

Frankfort meets my gaze, searching. I give him nothing because there is nothing to give.

We all take a deep drink. I am not sipping my usual Pussyfoot.

I reach into my satchel and pass a clean copy of *Thrown Away One Thoughtless Day* to Frankfort, whipped up admirably by Gemima in Effingham, who I have been out with on two separate occasions. Her company is quite charming. I also give my book of ghost and horror stories, titled *A Little Upside Down,* to Bertie. Both men are very pleased. Robert makes a crack, "where's my manuscript?" We laugh. I make my excuses and slowly walk back to Claridges.

I look at the Raymond Chandler book in my hand as I press the button of the intermains.

A voice crackles. "Password."

"Foxtrot. Oscar. Papa."

A pause.

"I'm sorry Mr Stickles, your membership has been revoked. You may keep the book you borrowed with the compliments of the club."

"Are you going to give a reason?"

"Goodbye, Mr Stickles."

I think back to the drunk, to what seems like a million lifetimes ago.

I hesitate, only for a couple of seconds, then speak into the intermains.

"You dirty *cunt.*" I have to force this alien word out. It sticks like vomit in my throat.

I press down hard on the buzzer then stand back a step with the book in my hand at an angle.

The door opens inwards, and there is orangutan man, his blonde hair clipped rather severely since I last had the pleasure to witness him at work. I bring the book down hard on his nose just as he sees me, his eyes widening in surprise and horror. His nose bursts in a gush of blood and I follow that with a foot planted squarely in his solar plexus and kick him off the stairs. From top to bottom he doesn't touch a step.

I run down after him, satisfied that he isn't going anywhere. His neck is broken.

It's not the girl serving, not the girl from last time, but a stocky bloke with a thick forehead and squinty eyes. I walk up to him and lob the book, which he catches. I punch his throat and he falls down hard.

I go to the door at the side of the room, the one where the drunk had been dragged through and do the same with the barman. He is an easy drag. It leads into a well-lit corridor and takes me to an office. The door is shut, opens easily. A woman, wearing a red sweater, obese, greasy hair and missing teeth is sitting at a table. She looks at me with fright.

"Who the fuck are *you*," she screams. She reaches across the table. I drop the barman, launch myself at her, grab her head with both hands and twist. It makes a pistol crack which is terribly loud in such a small room. She slumps to the floor, letting out a long, ragged death-breath. I see the gun, a WWII Luger she was looking to use. I chuckle. There is an open safe in the room, full of cash and ledgers. I take two cotton bags from the table, fill the first with cash, at least several hundred five pound notes and put the ledgers in the second. Crumpling up newspapers that are in a stack in the corner, I take a Zippo lighter and set fire to them, waiting till the flames take hold and a black plume of smoke fills the room.

Back in the bar I work quickly. I clear the shelves of books and pour several bottles of whisky over them. I use the Zippo once more and it goes up with a satisfying *whoomph*. I take the log book from the bar and run up the stairs and close the door until it clicks home, hard.

I walk quickly to Claridges, but don't ring the front bell. Instead I make my way to the servant's entrance. The door is still wedged slightly open, a ratty paperback against the door jamb. I put it into my pocket, continue my way through the deserted corridors and into the kitchen. Five steps to the ovens. Turn right. Three steps to the door. Out into the staff staircase. I run up it, barely breaking a sweat, a bag in each hand for balance. Once on the fourth floor, I peek around, and satisfied that there's no one there, creep gently back to my room.

Once the door is closed I lock it. I go to the window. The streets are completely deserted.

I look through the ledgers first. See my name, the addresses that I've stayed at, including Clemendy, and other bits of information about me that could only mean they had been spying on me when I was in Effingham. Bizzare. I think back to the person who sponsored my entrance into the club, one of the boys from my top secret days, Archie Kier. All they found of him was a shoe.

I spend the early hours tearing the pages from the ledgers into tiny squares. I'm surprised that I don't hear any sirens, but surmise that the wind must be blowing in the wrong direction. Once my task is finished I put all the pieces into paper bags which I then place in my suitcase.

I count the money. I am more than happy.

I'm not so stupid as to think that there may be other people in the shadows and they might have copies of the ledgers and will be making their way through the lists, looking for anomalies, looking for revenge. I could simply have a touch of paranoia, but my training of several lifetimes ago haunts me as much as Binky and mother used to.

The next morning I take the early train back to Effingham.

It is good to be back at Clemendy.

There has been a delivery. The postman knocks on the door and hands it over. It is the advanced copy of *Thrown Away One Thoughtless Day*. Dennis Wheatley and Graham Greene have kindly supplied lead quotes. Robert refused, saying he didn't know me well enough. Jealousy is an awful trait.

Britain's foremost post-war writer. Brave and bold.

A novel of unquiet depths. An honourable follow-up to his debut.

Frankfort has slipped in a letter thanking me again for trusting him with this 'important, important work' and that he's looking forward to my next novel. I put the book on top of *The Pan Book of Horror Stories* paperback that arrived the day before.

EPILOGUE

AS TO *THROWN Away*, I have yet to read the book. I'm sure it's a romp.

"... *his soul began to smile to itself*...'
—Patrick Hamilton,
Hangover Square

CHOKE

(1986)

"He's a devil, he's a devil
He's a devil in his own home town."
—'He's a Devil in His
Own Home Town'
Grant Clark and Irving Berlin

CALL

I TURN ON my brand new IBM PS/2, put a diskette in its drive and open up my current novel. It is called *Thx Dxxblx X* and is a departure from my usual fare. I am trying my hand at writing a different kind of crime novel. The idea originally came to me the year before when I was watching an episode of *The Bill* called 'Public and Confidential'. An officer with vertigo was sent up a high building to arrest some fellow who was throwing off roof tiles. In my novel he clambers onto the roof and meets a version of himself. I am happy with my progress although I cannot write like I used to. The days of being able to produce a short story on demand or write a novel in six months are long gone.

I get up and my back protests. I do not see eye-to-eye with old age, although people who knew me said that I was always an old head on young shoulders. I go to the kitchen and turn on the kettle. I make myself a cup of weak coffee, three sugars, and return to my writing desk. As soon as I sit down the phone rings. I let it ring out. I'm sure that they will ring again if it is important.

I drive into Effingham to pick up some meat from the butcher. I pass The Rita Hayworth and consider stopping in for a half. The pub has had three other names in the time I have lived here - The Sedentary Falcon, The Open Eye and Much Ado About Boozing, with that name and owner lasting less than six months.

"Ah, Mr Stickles, your usual?" the butcher, the delightfully named Arthur Bacon asks with a smile as I walk into the shop.

"Not today, I think I shall have a chicken breast and four sausages please. And a bone for soup."

"You're the only person that I know of who still uses the old methods," Arthur says, preparing my order. "You'll have to bring a little pot in one day so I can have a taste. I've tried to get my wife to follow your lead but she says it's too much hassle."

"That I can do," I say, having no intention of ever doing so.

"You opening the bookshop today?" he asks, passing the bag of meat over to me.

"No, I never open on a Monday."

I put the meat in the fridge, make myself another coffee and sit in front of the television and watch the one o'clock news. As much as I like to keep an eye on the world's events, I miss *Pebble Mill*. Damn the BBC, it really is going to the dogs.

The phone goes. As I am sitting next to it I pick the handset up on its second ring.

"Yes?"

"Hello, is that Russell Stickles?"

"Yes. Who is this?"

"Oh, hello Mr Stickles, my name is Robert Armstrong. I'm a researcher and historian. I write about literary indiscrepancies. Have you heard about me?

"I've seen you on the television."

"Thank you." He pauses. The line crackles. "Are you aware of an author called Thomas Caine? Had a single book published in the fifties called *Once Found, Always Found*?"

"I've not heard of that book," I glance up at Emilia's uncorrected proof copy of the book in my bookcase next to a partially-burnt edition of Steinbeck's *Grapes of Wrath*.

"Well," Robert interrupts, "a strange thing has occurred. A carbon copy of a manuscript was recently discovered in the stacks at a library in London, called *Thrown Away One Thoughtless Day* with Thomas Caine's name on it. Nobody has any idea how it ended up there, there's no paperwork with it.   I did a bit of research and discovered that you had written a book with the same title. Won several awards. I've got a copy."

"And you saw it was the same book," I grin. I hope that he can sense it.

"Yes. Have you got anything to say on the matter?"

"Of course I do, you didn't let me finish. You interrupted me. I originally wrote the book under a pseudonym, Thomas Caine. My agent, Herbert van Thal, discovered that there was already an author out there, deceased, may I add, by the time my book was written. It was decided to drop the name in favour of my own. If you've done your homework I'm sure that you've discovered the release of my second novel coincided with the publication of a collection of ghost and horror short stories. We were very hesitant in flooding the market with two very different works."

There is silence on the line. Then a cough.

"The copy is annotated. It's a rough draft. The annotations have made it into the finished manuscript which you passed off as your own. The handwriting isn't yours; I have several samples here. You've signed enough books in your time."

He has given me just enough rope with which to hang myself. He is good.

"You're not going to believe me if I tell you

that it was copy-edited?"

"I don't think that to be the case, Sir."

"Is this call recorded?" I hear an intake of breath, maybe a small curse. He is not *that* good.

"Very well, Robert Armstrong, I'll admit to it. The novel isn't mine. It *was* Thomas Caine's, and the story of how I came across it is very complicated. Why don't you come to Effingham? I'll bring the original manuscript that I discovered. Tell your bosses you'll be coming."

"This is an independent project. I've told no-one because I wanted this story to be concrete and to give you a chance to defend or explain yourself."

"How very admirable. Well, let's say we meet at a pub called The Rita Hayworth on Friday, 1pm. Or we can meet at my bookshop which is two doors down. It's called Binky's. I'll be bringing company, my carer. A lovely girl called Fiona. I don't get around as much as I used to."

I do not have a carer.

"That's fine."

Once I have hung up I toss *Once Found, Always Found* into the fire. I then go upstairs to the office and rifle through the filing cabinets until I find everything to do with *Thrown Away One Thoughtless Day*. The original manuscript, the copy Gemima made, contracts for paperbacks, foreign editions, film adaptations, audiobooks - they all party together in the hearth.

I pack a small overnight bag and phone a taxi to take me to London. I do not like driving lengthy journeys such as this.The train I need pulls in at Mercy, by the time I'd arrive I would miss the only train of the day that leaves from the station. I yearn for the days of the train from

Effingham. Dr Beeching and his infernal cuts. There is a station at Haven, but the line goes in the wrong direction.

CLUB

I ARRIVE AT the Reform Club at Pall Mall and am taken to my private chamber, the same one I have rented for overnight stays since the now sadly late Bertie van Thal got me in as a member all of those many years ago. I unpack my bag and place a clean pair of underpants, vest, shirt and a spare tie in the top drawer. I take off my blazer and sit by the window and close my eyes. The drone of the city below makes me doze. It's a pleasant sensation. When I wake I put in fresh contact lenses.

It is seven and as arranged, the receptionist, a cold fish who takes his job far too seriously approaches me and says that there is a Mr Barnard wanting to see me. I smile and ask him to be brought through. Mr Barnard is not his real name. Mr Barnard is not a friend, but we have entertained each other for the past thirty years. He is a criminal. I have used his criminal services on more than one occasion when I had problems I needed taken care of. He has used mine.

"Barnard," I stand and offer him a hand. He grasps it and smiles, and asks for a whisky and soda, one ice cube when the waiter arrives to take our order.

"Pussyfoot for me," I say, waving the waiter away.

"I'll never get your obsession with that drink," Barnard says.

"This is possibly the only place in the world where you can get one. I have never let them forget the recipe." I take a small sip. It is, as always, sublime. "The matter which is troubling me is a delicate one," I continue. "It involves a young man holding a rather nasty axe over my head, one that puts at risk these twilight years of mine. I would like to see the problem solved."

"Do you want him killed?"

"Nothing quite as vulgar as that, but I do want an accident that will reduce him to a vegetative state. However, before that I would like to be able to look around his house then have a chat with him. Can this be arranged?"

"When for?"

"Tonight."

Barnard looks visibly shocked. "I don't know who he is or . . ."

"Come now Barnard. I'm sure you have a warehouse you can take him to where his screams won't be heard by the good and sundry. And twenty thousand pounds in your pocket for one night's work surely can't be sniffed at."

Barnard deflates and shakes his head with a sly grin.

"He must have really upset you."

"Yes, he has. It is quite regrettable, really."

"Do you want an amphetamine?" Barnard asks. I nod and he fishes in his pocket and brings out a small brown bottle, unscrews the lid and tips a couple of pills out onto his palm. He gives me one. It has the number 3 on it. I dry swallow; it's small enough not to be an annoyance.

"He was relatively easy to find," Barnard says quietly. We are in his car, parked at the bottom of Long Street in Shoreditch. "My contact tracked him down in less than an hour. To be fair, when this does attract the attention of the police, it's no real problem. It appears that he's pissed off so many people in such a relatively short space of time that the Met will have a list as long as their arm to work from. And there he goes."

Barnard points to a man walking out of the alley between two houses. He carries the slumped Robert over his shoulder and puts him into an open van. The doors clatter shut, the headlights blink on and the van drives past us.

"Right," Barnard says, looking at me. "Your turn."

I get out of the car and walk to the alleyway the hired help emerged from. I walk down the vennell and to the gate, which is slightly ajar.

He certainly has done his homework. I am quite proud that I've been living in his head for so long. On his kitchen table is Caine's marked manuscript, and I think back to Emilia's room and the hole under the floorboard.

I search through the cupboards under Robert's sink and find a box of tealights. I place them around the table and light them, my hand shaking slightly. I then go to the cooker and twist the knobs for the burners and oven and open up the oven door. I am rewarded by an urgent hiss. I close the back door gently behind me and make my way back to the car.

"You really have outdone yourself with this place," I remark appreciatively to Barnard as we pull up at our final destination of the evening.

"Old textiles factory. There's a few bodies hidden around here. One famous fella's here too. That spot over there, by the ivy. Remember Henry Barry, the comedian? Making the ground very healthy with his nutrients." He holds his hand up to his temple, pointing with one finger. "One bullet to the head. Unpaid debts. Had enough of his bullshit in the end to be honest. He begged and begged. Even offered to give me his fucking Bafta! Going to give the police the runaround for months when they turn this place into flats." He giggles, a characteristic I find childlike and disarming.

"Yes, he used to turn up at the Reform every once in a while with Dennis Waterman. Never cared for him much myself so you did us viewers a favour, really. And what do you have planned for our Robert?"

"On your say-so, a few healthy smacks of a hammer. Not enough to kill him, but enough for him to be unable to feed himself."

"We really do bring out the worst in each other," I chuckle as we enter the building. We walk towards a distant low light.

CHOKE, PART ONE

ROBERT, LIKE THE victim in all gangster movies, is tied to a chair. The hired help stands off to one side.

"Hello Robert," I say, approaching him. "I'm Russell Stickles." Robert is wearing a hood over his head. I pull it off. He has a very angry bruise to his left eye.

He tries to scream but he is gagged. This is good; undue noise sets off my tinnitus.

"There's nobility in remaining silent and spending your last moments listening," I say, my mouth next to his ear. "So please do try. Nod if you understand."

He does. I put my hand on his shoulder. He flinches and starts to whimper.

"During the War I tortured a spy for days before she gave up her secrets. They weren't even that big a deal; we knew everything she knew beforehand. She was, however, the strongest person I've ever known. Normally, people will tell you anything you want to hear after the first day. In my experience you have to dig a little deeper to get to the truth. Something you failed to do, Robert. You dug, but you were unable to do due diligence, because my past doesn't officially exist. So when you came for me, you were never to know that I am . . . a problem solver."

I shout to the hired hand, "Can you bring me the length of rope from the car boot, please?"

And to Barnard, "can you please help me get Robert to a spot near that pillar?"

Robert squirms in his chair as we drag him across the concrete floor. The sturdy wooden legs make two trenches in the dust.

The help returns with the rope I asked for. I take a pair of leather gloves from my pocket, put them on. I then make a noose and drop it over Robert's head. I fashion a slipknot around the pillar. I push the chair forward, tipping him. The rope catches, is taut, bites around Robert's neck, crushing his windpipe. His hands, bound to the back legs of the chair, flex. I choke him for seven seconds then push him back. The chair rocks. He makes a rasping noise as he fights for breath.

"Does anyone have a knife?" I ask. Barnard looks at me, smiles and shakes his head. He passes me over a flick knife, something that the teddy boys would have had back in the '50s. I cut away the button from Robert's trousers and slice around his crotch. He is wearing boxer shorts, a frankly hideous trend in underwear. I reach my hand into the fly and bring out his penis. He squirms harder now.

"A long time ago a girl taught me how to walk the line between pleasure and pain. If you can walk this line, I'll let you go, you have my word. But I'll need to have your word that you'll never darken my door again, that as far as you and I are concerned, our account is closed. Do we have a deal?"

A nod of the head, *yes*.

"Good." I stand up and my knees pop like dry tinder. The first rush of amphetamine courses through me. I feel more alert than I have for at least a decade.

"Start pleasuring him," I say to the help. He protests to Barnard. I stand firm, putting my hands behind my back.

"Really?" Barnard says, taking a step towards me, his hands held up in a placatory measure. "This is a kink too far, old man."

I lob the knife with my left hand to Barnard, as he goes to catch it, my right hand comes from behind my back with a Colt Mustang, bought only the year before. I shoot him between the eyes. Thirty years or not, I simply don't have the patience I used to have.

He is dead before he hits the ground. The crack ricochets around the empty room. The help looks on in horror as I train the gun at him.

"Five more rounds," I say.

The help charges me but falls at my feet when the bullet goes through his eye.

I remove Robert's gag.

"Please don't do this," he moans.

I tip his chair forward. My tinnitus, as expected, enters stage left, jazz hands held high.

I fish through Barnard's pocket's for his car keys, take a roll of fifty pound notes from his pocket and slip off two gold rings. Robert has not stopped choking. The chair looks as if it will tip over by itself, but the rope is strong and Robert doesn't have the strength to try and rock himself back. Blood covers the concrete floor.

My heart hammers away in my chest like a budgie trying to escape its cage. I take a deep breath, try and slow myself down. I get into Barnard's car and drive away from the slaughter. When I'm a mile away, I stop, search the car. I find even more money alongside my brown bag of cash. I go to a phone box and place a call to 999, telling them, in a faultless Irish accent, where the body of Henry Barry can be found. I then drive off to Enfield, wipe the car down as best as I can, dump it down a backstreet, and leave the keys in the ignition. I get the night bus back into the centre.

BONDHAM

THE NEWS HAS not stopped going on about Henry Barry for days. *News at One. News at Six. Nine O'Clock News*. At times I regret phoning the police in the first place. The IRA are being blamed. They have surprisingly taken all the responsibility for Henry's murder and the many other bodies the police are digging up. This means that the police are working on a theory that Robert was working on a major IRA *exposé* and that his house was victim to a rigged explosion fits in with their theory.

I try to continue with my book but am losing the will to write it. It isn't progressing, I am stuck in authorial molasses. It is time for a holiday.

I decide on Worcester, in particular, Bondham. A journey to ghosts past, a place I always meant to revisit but never returned to since Emilia's demise.

There have been several women since Emilia. Gemima didn't care for the tastes her predecessor woke up in me. She got out as soon as she could. I found that as my earnings grew it was easier to have my needs taken care of by specialists in their field. Dominatrixes who would gladly choke you and keep their discretion.

While my days of narrowboating are over, I look through *Daltons Weekly* and find a reasonably priced Bed and Breakfast slap bang in the centre of the village. Once booked for the next day, I order a taxi to drive me to the train station at Haven – the train will take me to Birmingham, and then I can get another train from there to Bondham. I pack lightly, two pairs of underpants, a vest, two shirts, one pair of slacks and a thin jumper, lest the weather becomes chilly.

I try not to shiver as I watch a longboat make its way along the canal. The name of the boat is *The Nosferatu*, No. 1202. It is helmed by a young couple, impossibly beautiful. They wave and ask me how I am as they idle past. I retrace the journey and memories. The canal path seems to have become more overgrown, the trees more full. I think of Emilia, legs spread as I pleasured her. The way she flicked her head back with delight. The way the boat burned. I have not been troubled since that day.

I make my way to The Squirming Grub, looking at the delightful thatched building, but the name of the pub has changed. It's now the bland and boring Canal Inn.

"Bloody *hell*," I inwardly seethe.

A couple in their sixties walk past me and I nod as I glance at them. I decide against going into the pub, it will only make me impossibly angry so I slowly make my way into the village, taking in the smell of the wildflowers that line the hedgerows. Their smell is heady and delicious and slightly calms me down.

I stop in at the bed and breakfast to ask Ralph about local buses and take my medication, then make my way to the newsagents and buy a roll of Refreshers and two rolls of Parma Violets.

I am at Grave's End. I look up the hill. It seems steeper than ever before. I take it gently, zig-zagging my way up the road, the backs of my legs screaming out in protest until I get to the church. The door is locked. I laugh and sit down on the weather-worn bench by the church and eat a whole roll of Parma Violets. I watch the wheat in the field opposite sway slowly back and forth.

"Can I help you?" a voice asks me. I look up and the dog collar tells me it is the vicar. He is staring at me, his face weather-beaten and grey, the heavy bags under his eyes suggesting that he is not at peace with some part of his calling.

"I was just here to see Peter the Strangler," I say. "I read about him in a book not that long ago."

"I know the book you mean, I have a copy of it. Out of print now, of course. There was a time when we welcomed the notoriety and the money he brought in, but now, not so much. It seems that the only time people want to visit this place now is to rob us."

"Gosh, really? How awful."

"Yes, it's happened twice in the last five years. However, going back decades, local legend has it that a parishioner's grandfather died and left several gold sovereigns, two of which were to go to the church."

"The grandson, he didn't make it?"

"Oh, no, he got here fine, brought them to the church but couldn't find the vicar who was tending to one of the flock who was dying, so he popped them in the contribution box. Lo and behold, the box was broken into and emptied that night."

"Oh what rotten luck. And nobody was caught?"

"No, nobody ever is. The police don't care, the local station closed down fifteen years ago and what makes matters worse is it transpired that one of the coins could possibly be an extremely rare one, a King Edward Eight proof coin worth thousands in today's market."

An unexpected memory crawls through the

fog of time. I am trying my hardest to keep the smile from spreading all over my face. I put my hand into my pocket and bring out a ten pound note.

"Well, hopefully this donation will restore your faith in human kindness a little, it looks like you've been knocked around some," I say, offering the note to him.

"Oh thank you, ever so much, your generosity is very kind. I don't mind opening up and letting you see Peter the Strangler. Would be a shame for you to come this far and be denied."

I agree; to refuse now would seem off. He takes me to Peter's tomb, still unmarked by any errant vandal. No violence has been brought upon his resting bones. His are the remains that stay in their grave.

After I say goodbye to the vicar I walk back down the hill. I'm hot, soaked with sweat, and need to have a drink. I go into the shop and the girl at the till nods at me as I walk in. I grab a bottle of lemonade from one of the low shelves and give her its price and a little bit more. She smiles, her face revealing ugly, overlapping teeth. I instantly regret her tip.

I open the bottle outside and drink deeply. Once my thirst is slaked, I pour the rest out onto the ground and take the bottle back in. The girl looks at me, surprised, but gives me my deposit on the bottle.

I walk out of the village, my mind set on one thing. I walk to the last elm tree, just before the hedgerows. I try to remove one of the stones but it won't budge. I try another and a big brown spider runs up my hand and onto my arm. I flick it off. The stone comes out after some manipulation – moss has grown over it in the many decades since I was last here. The bag is there, completely brown with dirt and cobwebs. It jingles as I lift it out from the hole.

I open it up and look inside. A glint. I put my hand in and take out a gold coin. Turning it over in my hand I look at the date. 1936. My heart flips.

"So it *was* you all along!"

I look up. I don't recognise him. But again, an urgent memory. The longboat. Emilia wearing my shirt; his embarrassed look. He is fatter around the face, much fatter. He has not aged well. He must only be in his 60s. I look better than he does. Someone who had led a life of indulgent living and now in civilian clothes.

"I can't believe it's taken you this long to come back for them, to be honest," Monroe the policeman says. "We certainly didn't know there were sovereigns in amongst that lot, not until a few days later. And it looks like you didn't know either, otherwise you'd have come back a lot sooner. I always *knew* it was you, you were too *smooth*. And of course everything stopped when your lady died . . ." He leaves that hanging in the air.

"So, how do we play this, Officer Monroe?" I ask. "I take it your wife, if it was you and she who passed me when my head was elsewhere, is phoning someone?

"No, she's simply gone home. She doesn't know about you. I made an excuse. And it's not Officer. I had to leave, but left a Sergeant with a pension. One of the locals buried an axe in my head during a *fracas*. The station here closed shortly afterwards. I get headaches a lot. Couldn't hold down a steady job. I kept tabs on you though, you're a famous author, still to read any of your books, mind."

I smile. I take out the other gold coin and flip it to him. He catches it.

"If you can bear to join the ranks of the unclean, sell that and treat your wife to a little holiday."

He turns the coin over.

"Not the rare one, then." He grins and pockets his coin.

"No, not the rare one. I think if you tried to get rid of that round here there would be questions asked."

Monroe chuckles. "Yes, I think you might be right. I do hope you'll buy me a pint though."

"As long as it's not at the Canal Inn."

"No, I would never drink there, it's full of those bloody yuppies nowadays. If you like, there's a pub on the outskirts of town going the other way, called The Strangler's Arms, recently taken over and the owner wanted to jump on the local history bandwagon. It's a bit tacky, but they serve a good pint."

I nod. I am glad I do not have to kill Monroe. Saying that, I don't think it would actually take much of an effort.

We make our way to the pub. It's a gentle, meandering stroll and we do not say much. I moan every now and again as the walk up Grave's End catches up with me.

"I've not walked up that hill in years," Monroe says, chuckling away. "Why did you go up there this time?"

"Let me be straight about this. I totally forgot I misappropriated those church funds until the Vicar went on about the theft of the coins, and it came back to me. Your next question will be why. All I'll say is that I was simply bored."

"Bored? But you were with your girlfriend, I forget her na . . ."

"Emilia. She was never *boring*, but my tolerance threshold is very low. That's why you and I are only having one pint together."

Monroe chuckles again, an action he is clearly fond of. I am hit with a small pang of jealousy, it would be nice to spend life chuckling away, no matter the awfulness of life. Monroe has had more than his fair share of terrible sights and happenings.

"Are you happy here?" I ask him, sipping on my pint. I, for some unfathomable reason, asked for a lager. It is too cold and threatens to deaden my tongue.

Monroe takes a gulp of his bitter before replying.

"It's strange. When I had the job, I *was* the village. I was respected, people came to me with their problems, their first port of call. And times were much simpler back then, I'm sure you'd agree, even with all of the complications you found yourself in . . ." He looks at me but I do not answer as I am unsure as to what my reply would be. Were times simpler?

I think back to the last days of the war, in Germany, tracking down two of our spies with the sole aim of bringing them back home. I had no idea at that time if their cover had been blown or if they had been turned and were now working for the Nazis. Those days were stressful to say the least. But I did live my life to a code that I now miss. Kill or be killed. Survive or die.

"It was a simpler time, but the rot started to

set in. In 1961, I believe."

"Profumo?"

"For the country, certainly. Personally, I found myself in an asylum in '61. The doctors there believed it was the war and the death of Mother and Emilia catching up with me."

"I'm sorry to hear that you were stuck in there – to this day I believe they're still rather terrible places."

I take another drink of my beer. Perhaps I'll stay for another.

CLEMENDY

THE TAXI DRIVER drops me off half a mile away from home. It's a habit I've never been able to break since the war. Never get dropped off at your destination. Always survey the area around it. Approach cautiously.

I enjoy the walk. Walking is a pastime I don't do enough of nowadays, my bones sing weary songs and my recovery rate, especially after the journey up Grave's End, seems to be marked in multiples of days rather than a single day of muscle ache. My suitcase is strapped to a trolley so as not to be difficult to transport and the noise it makes as it trundles along the tarmacadam is deep and pleasing.

The first thing that I notice that is awry is that the gate is open. The postman, an erudite chap but one who does not believe in wearing pressed trousers, only shorts that come down to his knees, knows that it is imperative that the gate is closed on each and every occasion he pays the house a visit. If I am indoors the sound of the gate opening is the first sign that alerts me to someone visiting.

I push the trolley onto the verge and walk past Clemendy and slowly climb the gate in the field that runs parallel to the house. I walk low, my body covered by the stone dyke and let myself into the back garden. Here I take off my shoes, lifting each leg up and removing them slowly. I liberate the shoelaces from both shoes and tie them together.

The back door is open, only because one of the small panes is broken. I normally remove the back door key from its lock before leaving the house, but with age, you forget the smallest things.

Whoever it is is still in the house. I step carefully over the broken glass, it's localised so easy to navigate past. I slowly make my way out of the kitchen and up the stairs. The shoelace is taut. Luckily I have lost weight in the intervening years otherwise my footsteps would be heard, now I am silent if sloth-like. Whoever it is is in the bedroom. There is nothing of real value to be found unless they move the wardrobe and find the false door in the wall.

I creep in and there is the nuisance. They, for I cannot yet tell their sex, are kneeling at the chest of drawers. The top two are open. The third has still to be rummaged in. I drift across the room and skip the tied-together shoelaces over the intruder's head and around their throat. That they are wearing a hooded top of some sort will not protect their most vulnerable spot. I pull tightly and shift my weight and fall back onto the bed. They have no time to react, their hands go up to their throat, body freezing with panic. It is then I realise that I am not fighting against any weight. The struggle is almost the struggle of a child.

I let go of the lace with both hands at the same time and the intruder pitches forward and sits up.

It is a girl. She cannot be any older than twelve. Perhaps on the cusp of puberty. She cries and rubs her throat.

"You fucking psycho!" she screams. I am not concerned, there is no-one close enough to hear noise such as this.

"You were restrained for no more than three seconds, you'll have no lasting damage and the shoelace was not pulled tightly enough to rupture any small veins. You will not be marked. But you could have been," I say, my heart slowing back down to a more acceptable pace.

"I'm going to the police!" she yells, fury on her face.

"And why do you think I would ever allow you to do that?" I muse, a grin on my face. "Surely it should be me going to the police as you are the one breaking into my house and I have only tried to defend myself and my property. And what about your parents?"

A troubled cloud passes over her features.

"No."

"No what?"

"No police."

"Very well. Shall we have a cup of tea?"

This surprises her.

"I've just tried to rob you, mister."

"You don't have anything, for there is nothing to be found. At least have a cup of tea. It'll help with your nerves."

I get up off the bed and offer my hand. She grabs it and I pull her up. I let her leave before me, just in case she wants to make haste, but she goes into the kitchen and takes the kettle to the sink and fills it. Then she sits at the table and removes her hood. Auburn hair spills out.

"Nicola Cohen?"

She looks at me in panic.

"How did you . . ."

"It's okay," I raise a hand to pacify her. "You used to come into the bookshop with your father, he's Ted isn't he? Likes his railway books."

"Please don't tell him." She sounds broken.

"I won't. That much I will promise."

The kettle boils and I get up and make us both a cup of tea.

"How many sugars?"

"I've never had sugar in my tea before. I'm not allowed."

"Right you are, two it is then."

I turn to look at her and she gives me a weak smile.

"Aren't you going to ask me why I broke into your house?" she says after the first sip that takes her mouth by surprise, judging by the face she makes.

"No. It isn't any of my business. You have your reasons."

"But it's *your* house!" she exclaims.

"Yes. And it's nothing that a spare pane of glass and some putty won't fix. As soon as you're gone I'll place a call to the hardware store and then when I'm next in town I'll pick up everything I need and it won't cost that much to put right."

"You're strange, mister."

"Call me Russell, please."

"You don't have a wife? You live alone?"

"I had a wife a long time ago. She died."

"I'm sorry to hear that."

"It was . . . unexpected." A flash of Binky's mottled feet dance through my mind.

"Do you have anyone that helps out?"

"No, I manage pretty well on my own. Why are you offering to help me around the house a cool half an hour after you tried to rob it?"

Nicola's face turns beetroot.

"I'd like to go now, please," she mutters.

"You know where the door is. Watch the glass on the way out."

I take the dustpan and brush from the small cupboard under the stairs and kneel down and begin to sweep the glass up. Once collected I dump the glass in the bin outside and sit on the garden bench.

My suitcase.

I sigh and get back up and walk out onto the verge and wrestle with the trolley to get it back upright. Being old is no fun.

BOOKS

I BUMP INTO a pile of books and knock them over. I wince as they spill onto the floor. I don't swear, much as I want to, but I stare at them, and wait for them to either pick themselves back up or burst into flames. I look around me and not for the first time feel that I have built myself a prison. I think about the first day I opened up Binky's Bookshop and the steady flow of customers, some who came from as far away as Marn, Etchnard and Cardinal Moor. Today I opened up the shop merely to break up the boredom. I am lucky if I see more than ten customers in a week. I do not need the money; I have no rent to pay as I own the building. While I find comfort in books, I sometimes feel that as I have devoted the last thirty years to creating them, they now own whatever remains of my soul. I will never be able to escape them. I catch myself thinking these thoughts as I slowly pick up the books and put them on the desk. It is time for a cup of tea.

The bell rings as the door opens. I look up from my book, *The Woman Who Rides Like a Man* by Tamora Pierce. Fantasy books are not to my taste, but I have now read the first two books in the series. The first one came in as part of a consignment, I flicked through the first few pages and before I knew it I was along for a most enjoyable journey .

The customer is an unfamiliar face, but she is smiling. A woman and a child, I am presuming her own.

"Mr Stickles?"

"Yes?" My eyes do not leave hers. I am a

praying mantis. I am looking for any signs of attack. I find none.

"You might not remember me, but I'm Graham Roberts' daughter?"

I smile and get up.

"Angela, how could I forget? Well I *never*. It has been a long time. How are things and who is this delightful child?"

I walk towards her and we hug. Her child, a young boy, barely looks at me.

"This is my son, Billy," she says.

"Hello Billy, I'm Russell," I say, and hold out my hand. He takes it and for one so small his shake is surprisingly fierce.

"So what are you doing here? I really never thought I'd see you again after you all moved. Your father? Is he-"

"He passed five years ago, I'm afraid."

"I'm so sorry, I never heard. That's a real shame. He was a good man. I should know, he helped me out tremendously when Binky died and helped me get Clemendy."

"Yes, he was getting ready to do a Sunday service and he dropped dead five minutes before he was due to give it. Heart attack."

I find it strange that she would be so open about this in front of her child, to be so loose about the death of his grandad, but I say nothing and continue with my role as the sage old man.

"So what brings you back to Effingham? Holiday?"

"Divorce, sadly. And Mum wants to move back this way, she was really fond of the area, so I'm looking for a house for us all."

"That's splendid news. Have you seen anything you like?"

"Funnily enough, yes. You'll know of

Primrose Hildebrand's house?"

I nod.

"I was talking to the estate agent and they're having trouble shifting it, what with all of the unpleasantness that happened."

"Even in small villages you get the odd rotten apple." I remark. Effingham seems to have had more than its fair share.

"I know, but the Doctor? Did you know him?"

"I was in need of his services once or twice, but apart from that I didn't know him. Who would have guessed he'd kill Primrose?"

I want this to end. Idle gossip isn't my thing at all, but Angela seems as if she needs to drink until she regurgitates.

"So, are you going to buy it?"

"We've put in an offer. I thought I'd treat Billy with a couple of books. Do you have anything he might like?"

"Have you heard of Alan Garner, young man?"

"No."

"Well, he's one that you'll like. He's visited the shop a few times in the past. Now where is it?"

I go to the stacks and rummage about until I find it. A first edition of *Weirdstone of Brisingamen*.

"Here we are!" I show him the cover of the hardback, a hirsute man holding a red glass.

"If you like wizards and evil sorceresses this is the book for you. And if you don't, you soon will. It's a book that will blow your mind," I tell him.

"How much?"

"No charge," I tell Angela, waving my hand at her. "Call it a housewarming present for him. And look at it this way, if he wants the sequel, he'll have to buy it!"

"Thank you," Billy says, taking the book from me. "I'll start reading it tonight."

I lock the door of the shop and pop over to 'Eggs and Ham in Effingham', a delightful little place that opened up last year, and order a bacon, lettuce and tomato sandwich. I bristle when the high-haired waitress corrects me and calls it a BLT. I have no time for acronyms. The sandwich is good, the tea just as I like it. I spend a whole hour in Eggs, I take my time, order myself a walnut cake and another pot of tea. I chew over the events of the past few weeks. A trip to London will be in order to get rid of the King Edward coin. While I don't believe Monroe would tell tall tales, he is now, of course, complicit in his own way. I believe that he is too partial to the drink and loose lips sink ships, as everyone was fond of saying during the war. I need to think. Maybe I was too hasty in dealing with Monroe, believing that a few pints would buy his silence.

I wander back over to the shop and reopen.

"You have turned breaking into properties I own a habit," I say to Nicola as I close the door behind me.

"You left the back door open this time, I *promise*," she said, smiling benignly. "I made you a cup of tea."

"I've already had several cups, at this rate, I'll be going to the toilet for the rest of the day," but I take the cup off her and sit at the desk.

It is then I notice the discolouration under her left eye. It is turning yellow, the colour of dying wheat.

"Who hit you?" I ask bluntly.

"My dad. I've not been back at home for a couple of days now."

I am disheartened that my initial thoughts of him have been proven right. A most distasteful chap.

"Where have you been sleeping?"

"There's an old garage on the Haven road, there's a mattress in there—" she breaks off, her bottom lip trembling. She is not my concern. My next words surprise me.

"Would you like me to buy you a sandwich?"

She nods yes. She does not look at me.

"I can't pay you back, Russell."

"Don't be foolish. I can afford it." I bring out my bi-fold wallet, the same one I have had since the '50s – it has only needed one repair. I pull out a pound note and pass it to her.

"Go get yourself something hot."

She takes the note and leaves the shop and I see her cross over the road and go into Eggs. I take my cup of tea through to the small kitchen at the back, indeed I did leave the door unlocked, and pour the cup down the sink.

I watch Nicola through the wide window as she looks this way and that before crossing and I don't want her to come back into the shop, but I know she will. She has found herself a haven. We are both about to find out whether it is a temporary one or not.

"You can sit at the table," I tell her as she re-enters. She has a pasty of some description and a can of coke.

She starts to eat, flakes of pastry falling down onto her top. She apologises through a mouth of food and stands up and walks carefully to the bin and brushes the crumbs into it. She then picks up the bin and sits back down, using it as a catch-all.

"When will you go back home?"

"Tonight. Dad's going away tonight, he goes away every weekend."

"What does he do?"

"The trains, he goes around the country taking photos of them."

"And your mum? Does he hit her?"

"Yes. And she hits me too, but only when he hits her."

"Do you have any aunts and uncles you could go and stay with? The summer holidays have just started, you could have the next six, eight weeks away from them if you wanted."

"I have an auntie who adores me, my mum's sister. She lives in Scotland though. I don't think my mum or dad would let me go up there on my own. He's always saying that he doesn't trust me and that I'm a slag -"

"Please don't use that sort of language, it's unbecoming. You've no need of it."

"And that I have a lot of boyfriends. I'm only thirteen. I've not even *kissed* a boy yet." Nicola starts to cry. I will not comfort her.

I put my hand on her shoulder to comfort her.

She sobs quietly and I stand there waiting for the tears to trail off.

"I don't open the shop every day, but if you see it open, you're more than welcome to keep me company. You can put some books on the shelves and help around a bit."

"Really? You'd do that for me?" Her face shines with thanks and relief. She gets up, I think, to cuddle me. I hold my hand to stop her, *no*.

"We can start now. I'm going to go and pick up some things for my dinner tonight, those piles of books there, they all need to go into the history section which is down that side corridor. Alphabetical order, please. I'll be checking so no shortcuts."

EXPLOSION

I STAND AT the toilet and try to urinate. The window is slightly ajar so I can see into the garden. It is early morning and already looks as if it is going to be a 'mad dogs and Englishmen' type day. Finally my bladder gives up and releases a weak stream. Once finished I flush the toilet and wash my hands with coal tar soap. I dry my hands on a newly-bought St. Michaels towel. I find a heavy-weight cotton   much softer for my hands, even though it takes longer to dry them.

I will open the shop today. It has been a week since I last opened it, mainly to force Nicola back home. I do not want to offer her false hope that she can use the place like the youth centres that seem to be growing like mushrooms in the area.

I put on my vest, shirt and slacks. I grimace when I go to put on my shoes; they pinch my feet and I find that I'm in pain less than half an hour after putting them on. I rip them from my feet and throw them across the floor. I put on my Dunlop trainers instead. They are much more comfortable. It is strange, I find that they incite derision from teenagers if I happen to walk past them. I find their mocking funny. I wonder how they would have coped during the war.

I open up the shop and pick up the mail. I open the first letter and see that it is from Richard Dalby, a lovely chap who is into his ghost and horror books. It is quite difficult to talk to him on the telephone as he has a severe stutter, but once you get him on a subject that he is passionate about, the stutter seems to vanish and you are faced with one of the most knowledgeable people

I have ever known. He says that he would like to interview me about my career and my friendships with Aickman (with whom he had a mutual friendship), van Thal and Dennis Wheatley. As Dennis has been dead for almost ten years by this point I really want to tell him about the things that we got up to in the war, but I believe that I am still bound by the official secrets act and that our exploits will not be unveiled until 2015, or some ludicrous date like that – long after I am worm food.

I have often toyed with the idea of 'spilling my guts' and going to the press or writing a very limited autobiography on that window of war from thirty-nine to forty-five. The more I think about what I was, what I was made to be, what I did and how I did it often spins me into a sharp melancholy that can last for months. It certainly coloured my time with mother and Binky – and completely exhausted me when I was with Emilia. It certainly contributed to my time in the asylum and even today at seventy-four years of age, gives me pause for thought. My first instinct is to attack and destroy. Then I pretend to heal by swallowing medication that more often than not slows me down.

It is better to keep my exploits to myself. It would only cause people to dig. I hate it when people tell me they are digging.

The phone goes. It is someone asking me if I buy books.

"Of course, this is a bookshop."

"Can I bring them in? They were my grandad's."

"What kind of books are they?"

The person on the other end hangs up. It could be that I will be sailing into occupational hazard territory, when I tell someone who has driven many miles to the shop with a car full of books that the ones they have brought to me are not the kind of books that I am looking for and that they would be better off giving them to a charity shop or to look in the newspapers for the next 'bring and buy' sale and try their luck there.

The doorbell goes. I wander through to the front of the shop. It is Nicola. She is dressed presentably. It is a far cry from how she normally looks.

"You've not been open for the past few days," she says.

"No, I couldn't be bothered opening. I am trying to write a new book and I thought that time away would be time better spent."

"And was it?"

"No, I didn't write a thing."

We both laugh.

"Cup of tea?" I ask.

"Two sugars."

We are chatting away over our drinks. It is our third cup each. We are not getting much work done. Nicola, for all of her housebreaking tendencies, seems to be a thoroughly decent person. I do not normally like to spend more than an hour with anyone nowadays, but she is somehow able to pierce through my rather staid defences with abrupt and direct questioning. I have no choice but to answer her questions.

"Why haven't you married again?"

"I find women tiresome."

"When were you last in love?"

"Define love."

"You're a fool, Russell."

"Thank you for reminding me."

I am finding her company useful. It elevates my spirits. I am no longer going back to the house feeling down. I admit that I have been lonely for a long time and have yearned for someone to talk to me. I admit I haven't made it easy for anyone to get close. I have issues that nobody finds out about until it is too late.

I hope that I never have to kill Nicola. I have a feeling it would aggrieve me somewhat.

"What did you do in the war?" Nicola asks. We are eating Eccles cakes and drinking a cup of coffee, Maxwell House.

"I don't really know if I should tell you," I say slowly. She's a child – the fists that she's felt from her father is more than enough to let her know about the evil that men do. I feel that the mundanity of evil men is too much for a girl who has entered puberty.

"You killed people." This is a statement.

I pause.

"Yes."

"As a soldier? You don't look the type."

"That's what made me good at my job."

"Were you a spy?"

"I discovered secrets. I broke spies who tried to hurt our country."

"Break them? How do you break someone? You can't break people."

"Would you like me to show you?"

I have cleared the books off the desk. I have brought through another chair from the kitchen. This is the chair that Nicola sits on.

"Now, obviously, I'm not going to harm you, but the instant that you get scared, tell me and we'll stop."

"You're not scary. My *dad* is scary."

I stare at her and know that a couple of sentences will easily break her. I also have to be aware of our surroundings, we are clearly visible from the street.

"I want you to think of a secret, something only you will know. Something that you have locked deep into your heart. It has to be the truth, otherwise this is pointless."

"I have a secret." Her face is slightly troubled. She closes her eyes.

"Would your father be angry if you told anyone about his . . . handling of you?"

"When he hits me?"

"When he visits you in your bed."

"No . . ."

"That's because you push it down so deeply it won't trouble you. But it's always there, always a part of you. You fear him when he's had a bit too much to drink and your mother's crying downstairs. Because she *knows* it's *your* turn. He tells you that he *loves* you. But someone who loves you would *never* do that"

Nicola's eyes snap open.

She breaks.

"What he does to you is illegal," I say gently. Nicola is sobbing into a tissue. She looks at me, anger on her face.

"And do what? Go to the police? Nobody would believe me. My dad is very convincing. And my mum would back him up. And what after? If I did tell the police and nothing happened? Dad would make sure—"

The bell above the door goes.

"Nicola, what the fuck are you—"

A man, brown hair, green eyes, monobrow

and stubble comes into the shop. Nicola freezes, stares at me in fright.

"Mr Cohen, what a pleasure it is to see you again," I say as I get up.

Ted doesn't appear to be aware that I exist.

"Where have you been, you little *cunt*," he snarls and grabs Nicola by her hair. He yanks her up, she screams and hits at his arm for him to let go.

I open the drawer of the desk and grab the letter opener. I walk towards him and stab him in the hand, just deep enough to give him pause. He looks up. It is a look I have seen many times before. Pure, unadulterated fury. He pushes Nicola to the ground.

"And who the fuck are you and what are you doing with my daughter?" he says menacingly. I smile.

"I'm merely looking out for her."

"You dirty old man, you wanting to fuck her, is that it?"

"No, I think you're the only one doing that to her, Ted."

Ted roars and crashes into me, and the letter opener flies out of my hand. We go across the room and I slam into a bookcase. I fall to the ground and as the books tumble his fist follows me, a punch to the head. Another, another.

OLD

I WAKE UP. I sense the space around me. I am not at home. I hear the low drone of people talking to the left of me. I try to open my eyes but am unable to. They feel like they are super glued shut. It is then the pain hits me. I cry out and try to move my arms to give myself some protection, some comfort.

"Hello Mr Stickles," a soft male voice says. "You're in Effingham General. You've had a bit of an accident."

"The girl?" I ask.

"I don't know anything about a girl, I'm afraid. A relative? You were found by a passer-by. You fell and crashed into a bookcase, I believe."

"How bad is it?"

"You've broken an arm, two ribs and badly broken your hip on your left side. That's been replaced. Do you have anyone we can call? Any relatives?"

"No, I live alone."

I feel a hand comforting me, stroking my upper arm.

"You'll be able to see once the swelling has gone down. You're very lucky to be alive. I'll give you something for the pain and you try and get back to sleep."

I wake up, it is light. I try to open my eyes and discover that my left acquiesces. I have been moved, I am now in my own room. I move my head around, and doing so causes a sea-sick lurch so I stop. I wait for someone to come and tend to me.

"Hello Mr Stickles, how are you doing, it's me Angela."

"Oh hello!" I try to get up, but pain stops me. "What are you doing here?"

Angela comes in and cuddles me gently. She smells of expensive perfume.

"Hello Mr Stickles, it's Billy. Are you okay?"

"I'm a bit sore if truth be told. How did you find out about me?"

"It was us that found you. We were in town, viewing Primrose's house again and Billy wanted to buy you a cake. We saw the lights were on in the shop and came over. We managed to get the bookcase off you—"

"Lucky it wasn't one of the heavier ones," I say and chuckle. This causes my ribs to tell me off.

"You were barely breathing. We were really worried about you."

"Well I owe you both a great deal of thanks for rescuing me. You didn't happen to see a father and his daughter nearby did you? I remember them being in the shop before it all happened."

"Sorry, no." Angela has pulled up a chair and has placed a shopping bag on my bed. From it she takes a bag of grapes and a bottle of Lucozade.

"Have you got a mirror?"

"A small compact, why?"

"They haven't let me see my face yet."

"It's really bad," Billy says.

"Billy!" Angela admonishes him.

"Sorry, but it's true!" Billy continues.

I laugh, another stab of pain as reward.

"It's fine, let the boy be."

Angela removes a compact from her bag and opens it, holding it out to me. I take it with my good right arm and look at my face. Although I can now see with both eyes, the pupils are heavily bloodshot. My face is purple and bloated. My bottom lip is split in three places, making drinking a chore. Ted certainly had his fun.

"Gosh. I look rather mangled, don't I? Like I've been in a car crash."

"How are you going to manage when they let you out of here?" Angela asks as I hand the compact back.

"With some difficulty, I imagine. But I don't think I'll write myself off just yet," I shrug, and again, a tweak from the ribs. "How long has it been since I last saw you?"

"Two weeks now, and the reason we're here is to sign the papers for Primrose's house. I've bought it."

"Oh that's really good news. When do you move in?"

"Officially, as soon as the solicitors do their thing, however the movers are scheduled for a week Thursday. We've moved into a bed and breakfast on the outskirts of town in the meantime. You're not really enjoying it, are you Billy?"

"No. I do like the book you gave me though, Mr Stickles. It's such a good story. I'm going to be really sad when I finish it."

"Well remember there's the sequel, which I have a copy of in the shop. Once I get things back to-"

"Let me get the shop back to normal for you," Angela says. She reaches out and touches my hand gently. "At least let me tidy up the mess."

"No, I couldn't let you," I admonish. "It was stupid fool me who fell over, it should be stupid fool me that tidies it up."

"The place looks as if it's been robbed when

you look through the window, and you're not going to be in any fit state for a while to do anything about it. Hand over your keys."

She will not take no for an answer. She holds her hand out and her face is set.

I nod my head towards the drawer next to me.

"In there, separate them from my house keys."

I am alone. I think about killing. I have lived with my trade since I was a teenager. I cannot say that it has been an easy one to live with. In the years after the war and specifically after the trilogy of deaths – Mother's, Binky's and Emilia's I spent several years in an asylum. I was told that my mind was slightly mis-wired. The doctors said it was no doubt due to the excessive trauma of witnessing these deaths. The doctors, of course, were fed on what I allowed them to eat. If truth be told I suppose my 'mis-wiring' is what has driven me on to do what I did. I try to count the number of deaths I am responsible for. I give up after eighty.

I think about Ted. I am going to have to be extremely careful. It will take time for me to heal and I do not know what harm he is doing to the child. I do not know why I want to protect Nicola from him. I see *something*. I see something in *her*. I believe that it might be a case of type recognising type. She is cut from the same damaged cloth as I. She does not yet, however, have the capacity or temerity to take the first step on her road of self-discovery. I can help her. I will help her. I do not want my experiences to die with me. My skills were hard-learned. To let them die with me would be a waste.

I think about Angela. She can be used. She can be made to fall in love with me. It will confuse her, it might even disgust her to begin with, the thought of being with someone thirty-odd years older. But she will slowly accept it. It is something to think on. That she is fixing the shop is good. She has invested in me.

I think about the future. Things will get very dark and bloody. My favourite hues.

I ask the nurse to wheel through the telephone so I can place a call with my solicitor. Marcus Murphy. A natural born blusterer. It is his style, and I have always ignored it. I ask him to visit me at the hospital as I would like to amend my will. We make an appointment for Friday. Today is Wednesday. I close my eyes and think about Ted. I want it to be very special as I do not think I will survive.

CHOKE, PART TWO

I LEAVE THE hospital, the taxi driver taking my bag for me. I heavily favour the walking stick that I have been given. I have been told that I will not need the stick forever, but it will be a useful prop for when I am back in full health. I do not, however, like the cheapness of it. I will buy myself a cane as soon as I am able.

The taxi driver is a talkative chap. I surprise myself by being equally as talkative. I think that perhaps the long stretches of solitude I endured in the hospital are different to the long stretches of solitude I enjoy at home. We talk about what's been happening in town, and I am rather surprised that the Mayor has been caught with his pants down. Maurice Gilman would be the last person on earth you'd think would have a mistress. He looks like a choked toad.

We drive through the countryside. I drink my surroundings in. I allow myself to be dropped off outside Clemendy. It is good to be back home. I give the taxi driver a generous tip and he helps me take my bag to the front door. I open the door and push through the pile of letters and junk mail that has accumulated since my hospitalization. I step over the threshold carefully. The taxi driver comes into the house and puts my bag on the floor next to the telephone table. I protest, but he picks up all of my mail. I ask him to put it on the kitchen table for me. He is more than happy to oblige. Once we part ways I shut the door and make my way into the lounge and lower myself onto the 'comfy' chair, my hip only protesting slightly. I rest the walking stick against the fireplace and close my eyes.

I wake. It is dark. I reach out with my left hand, find that I am unable to, I have forgotten that it is still in a sling. I try to sit up, it takes a while as my lower half feels as if it has still to wake up. After several minutes of labour, I manage to put on the lamp. I reach for the stick and manage, after some trouble, to get up. I don't think that I will be able to sit in the chair for a while yet, if this is the trouble it is going to give me.

I look at the clock on the mantelpiece. It is 9pm. I walk through to the kitchen, put on the kettle and sit at the table and make my way through the mail. I come to an envelope with 'Russell' written on it in a childish hand. I rip it open.

Russell,

I am very sorry what my dad did to you. Life has got much worse, he beats me up all the time and asks me if you are my boyfriend. He has stopped going on his railway journeys because he says he doesn't trust me, but still has to work so I managed to leave the house to post this. My mum is hitting me more too. She is drinking all of the time now. I really hope that my dad did not hurt you too badly. I have not been able to find out from anyone. You are an old man and you do not deserve what he did to you. I hope you can find it in your heart to forgive me. I am so scared I do not know what to do. I hope to see you soon.

Nicola ♡ X ♡

I put the letter down and make myself a cup of tea, two sugars. I go into the fridge and realise that the half-pint of milk in there is off. I pour it down the sink, marvelling at how thick and lumpy it has got. The smell does not bother me, there has been worse. I run the tap and break the lumps up with my good hand. I take two paracetamol and then go out into the garden. Dark shadows comfort me.

It is 4am. I am still awake. The radio is on, a low drone. I am upstairs in my office. I am not at the IBM, that remains switched off. I am on my typewriter, typing away with one hand. It is slow and very laborious. I am not writing *Thx Dxxblx X* – I now consider this an abandoned novel. It does not interest me. I have decided to write my autobiography, as much as I am able to. I will of course leave out bits that may cause raised eyebrows. My habitual thieving, Binky's suicide, my exploits with Barnard, etcetera, etcetera. I have decided that my main focus will be on the war, especially the last year when I was smuggled into Germany to bring back our undercover agents. There are many things that the British public do not know and should know about what happened during those dark days.

THE SPY-BREAKER
RUSSELL STICKLES

PROLOGUE

You will be reading this book sometime after 2015, seventy years after WWII ended. I will be long dead. I am seventy-four years of age at the time of writing my memoirs. One or two of you may know me through reprints of various novels and collections that I have had published.

However, by the time that this book comes round I will be an obscure footnote in British literary fiction.

There have been many journalists and many other curious folk over the years who have asked the question: "what did you do during the War" and I told them that I was a conscientious objector. Some journalists who interviewed me during the Falklands conflict (I think around the time HMS Sheffield was destroyed) were sympathetic to the stance that I took. Others felt that I was not patriotic. I remember the late Harold Puckett of The Sunday Times who reviewed my latest book as "written by a coward."

As much as I wanted to answer him at the time, I held my tongue. The truth is that I played a very active part in the war and while I am unsure of what official records there are, they are out there. As far as I, and my superiors were concerned, I did not officially exist. My part played during the war was to make sure that spies gave up their secrets. I was what is known as a 'spy breaker' and I was very good at my job. Near the end of the war I was sent to Germany by a splinter-group of the London Controlling Section to bring our spies back – some were deep undercover and their lives were in great danger as Berlin crumbled.

I have read the many books that have come from the leaders of war over the decades and I remain frustrated at the lack of honesty on our part and what we had to do to win the war. Torturing of spies was par for the course. In his 1957 book, The London Cage, *Alexander Scotland denies that the torturing of spies ever took place there. This is completely and categorically untrue. I know this because I played my part in the torturing of a spy there called Bettina Jarzinck. In fact, I had a bet with Scotland as to how long it would take me to break her. Scotland isn't here to defend himself, he has been dead for twenty years. This is the reason I will instruct my solicitors when my bones are dust. Maybe enough time will have passed for the National Archive to release more files and documents on what happened during the war. Maybe the London Cage will give up its ghosts. This old ghost is giving up his.*

Russell Stickles, Clemendy, Effingham-on-the -Stour. 1986

I wake seconds before the gate opens. The letterbox snaps. The gate closes. Either the postman is very early or I have slept in. I fear that it is the latter. I get out of bed slowly, my new hip making its presence felt and I go to the toilet, without my stick to aid me, to urinate. I stand there for five minutes, trying to will myself. As hard as I urge, nothing happens and I give up.

I get dressed quickly, this means no vest. I gingerly make my way down the stairs. I cannot hold the bannister on the way down as it is my left arm that is broken. I have to tuck my stick under that arm and use my right hand to use the wall as my guide. It is all very bothersome.

There is a single envelope on the floor, face down. I groan as I pick it up. I turn it over, there is no stamp, no postmark, just my name in that childish handwriting. I unlock the door and go out into the front and look for her. I shout her name. I wait there for five minutes calling for

Nicola to come to the house, but she does not. I close the door behind me and walk into the kitchen and pull a knife out of the drawer and open up the envelope.

Russell,

You have been good to me. I would like you to know that this is goodbye. I think it's best if the whole world was rid of me and it will stop all of my pain.

Nicola ♡ X ♡

I stare at the letter. I wonder if I should rip it up and let her get on with the last few remaining moments of her life. I find that I cannot.

I phone the taxi company to have them send out a car, but I am told that there is at least an hour's wait for one to be sent round. I go to my bag which has yet to be unpacked and I rummage around in it until I find a scrap of paper with a telephone number written on it. I take a deep breath and dial the number. This is not something I want to do.

"Effingham 61230, A—"

"Angela, it's me, Russell. Can you help me?

She can sense the urgency in my voice.

"What's wrong, have you fallen?"

"No, there's someone I know, I believe that she's about to harm herself. We *need* to find her."

"Can't you go to the police?" Her tone is curious.

"Right now, no. Possibly if we find her. I cannot get a taxi."

"I'm sorry Russell, I'd love to help you but I

can't, I'm off to the hospital."

"What's happened?"

"Billy, he was climbing the coal shed in the dark last night and broke both his legs. I'm only here to pick some things up for him. Phone me later, okay?"

I slam the phone down in its cradle.

"Fuck!"

I phone the taxi company and tell them to send a car round as soon as they can. I put on my shoes, grab my spare set of bookshop keys and wait outside for the car to arrive.

I ask the driver to take the long way into town. My thinking is that Nicola would want to cut through the woods and go through the park and out onto the north side of town. We do not see her. I am dropped off at the shop. I ask the driver if he can come and pick me up at 6pm. He says he won't be working then, and that I should book the taxi as soon as I get into the shop. I do as I am told and book myself a car.

I am impressed with the job that Angela has done. The bookcase is back in its position and looks to have been screwed into the wall. All of the books that were on the table are gone, no doubt to their correct sections. There is absolutely nothing for me to do but wait. At lunch I hobble over to Eggs and order a sausage bap and take it back to the shop. I eat a bite, but I do not feel hungry. An unusual worry upsets my stomach.

The odd customer comes into the shop and we talk about my accident and how I'm doing. I am cordial and pleasant, and I wish I could turn the sign for it to be 'closed' but if Nicola walks past I want her to know that she can come in. That she will be safe.

At five I go to the grocery store and buy a few items for dinner. When the cab arrives an hour later I regretfully close up shop and go home.

The radio is on.

"The body of a young girl was found this morning . . ."

"The body has been named as Nicola Cohen. Police are not looking for anyone else involved in her death and are treating it as suicide. She was thirteen years old. Her headmaster . . ."

"The funeral of Nicola Cohen, the teenage girl who hanged herself at Downpit Woods last week, took place this morning at Effingham Parish Church . . ."

I phone Marcus Murphy and tell him that I will need to change my will again. He does not ask questions because he is paid not to.

I wish Mr Barnard had not been so flighty and that he was still with us. He would have been useful in this type of situation. There are other people I can get a hold of, but none I trusted as much as Mr Barnard.

OLD DOG, OLD TRICKS

I AM ON the train. I drink from a cup of sweet tea. I watch the countryside zip by. I am on my way to London. The ticket inspector takes my ticket and punches it. The sound feels good. Final. I sit at a table. On the other side is a young man. He reads a hardback copy of *A Confederacy of Dunces* by John Kennedy Toole. The front cover is an illustration of a large man wearing a deerstalker, carrying a scimitar in one hand and a hotdog in the other. It is not a book that has come through my door as of yet.

"Is your book any good?" I ask the reader.

He puts the book down and looks at me, sees that I am not threatening, genuinely interested.

"Yes, I think it's one of the best books I've read for a long time. It has even won the Pulitzer Prize for fiction. "

"May I ask what it's about?"

"Of course. A character called Ignatius J. Reilly tries to find work in New Orleans, but he's basically a fat and lazy Don Quixote."

"And the author?"

"Killed himself because the book kept on getting rejected. It was his mother who persevered and found a home for it after his death."

"Writing is subjective."

"Genius is objective." He raises the book. "This book is a work of genius."

"I'll have to take your word for it, I will say that it certainly looks meaty. If I were to give you forty pounds for it, right now, would you sell it?"

"Are you serious?"

I reach into my jacket and bring out my

second wallet. From it I take out two twenty pound notes and place them on the table in front of him. His eyes widen. He looks at me as if I am mad. I can see that he has reached the conclusion that I probably am.

"That's a deal, mister!" He takes the money without looking at the notes. He will be very upset when he realises that they are fake.

The young man gets off three stops after our transaction.

I check the book, it is a US first edition and it is in very good condition. There are no interior pencil or pen marks so it has not come from a second-hand dealer. I am sure that it will be worth quite a bit.

I get up carefully as the train pulls into London Liverpool Street. I retrieve my bag and stick from the holder above and put the book in it. I take my time getting off the train. I have my ticket ready at the barrier. I give it to the inspector who smiles me through. I get into the first available taxi and ask to be taken to the Reform Club. I made them aware the day before that I would need my chambers prepared for my arrival.

I take the book out and put it in the drawer alongside my underpants and socks. I freshen up and go downstairs and order a pussyfoot, as tradition dictates. At seven I ask for a cab to be ordered to take me to a pub called The Bear in Whitechapel. We drive alongside the Thames, past Cleopatra's Needle and turn up before Tower Bridge, through Aldgate and into Whitechapel.

The Bear is a pub inhabited by scum, but the best kind. It is a place I have used on and off since its opening in 1969. I have dressed down for my visit; my blazer is shabby, my shoes have been allowed to lose their shine.

"Russell, over here," I am hailed as soon as I step over the threshold.

A man, as old and as grey as I am, stands up. Sitting next to him is a man in his forties with long black hair.

"So very good to see you again Philip," I say, shaking his hand.

"What's with the stick?" Philip Lord asks.

"I'll tell you after you buy me a pint."

"Done."

Philip makes his way to the bar and the man with the long black hair looks at me.

"So you knew Dad during the war then."

"Yes, that's correct."

"Was he as much of a pain as he is now?"

I chuckle.

"No, I do believe that I was the pain in our partnership and most probably the source of his grey hair. Did he tell you that we were in Germany together right at the end?"

"That you got him out?"

"Yes, he was in deep cover in Berlin. We had a chance to get him into Hitler's bunker, but as soon as we did his cover was blown and I had to get him out."

Philip's son looks amazed.

"He never told me that," his voice full of awe.

"We weren't there to kill Hitler or anything, but we were trying to get hold of some files that we believed mapped out where the top-brass Nazis were all going to be fleeing to. If we had managed to hold our nerve for ten more minutes we would have sorted them all out long before they established their rat runs and buggered off to Argentina."

"Right, here's your pint," Philip says, joining us.

"Dad, you didn't tell me you were in Hitler's bunker!" his son admonishes him.

Philip rolls his eyes.

"So, you've told Jake then? Loose lips sink ships, Russell! I'm never going to hear the end of this now, am I? He's forever going to be going on at me to tell him about it." Philip says this in a good-natured tone so I know that I have not overstepped the mark.

We drink and reminisce. Jake interjects every so often with an easy to answer question. The bar is busy and as the hours tick by, less so. Philip then says we should move onto another place.

We walk to another place, five minutes away. The drink has made me feel loose, my steps are more adventurous, I am less reliant on the walking stick.

We arrive at a pub called The Dying Moon and instead of sitting in the bar area, go through a closed door at the back and up a flight of stairs. My hip bites at this point and Philip and Jake wait for me at the top of the stairs. Once I catch up with them we go through into a room. It is near-empty, but at the far corner there is a man sitting with a glass of what looks to be whisky in front of him. He has straw coloured hair and a face that's near-taken over by a big moustache. It's impressive. And he somehow remarkably pulls it off.

Philip tells Jake to stay back and we approach him.

"Philip, is this him?" The broadest of cockney accents.

"Yes."

"Sit down then, Russell. And fuck off Philip."
Philip does as he is told and he and Jake both go
back downstairs.

I sit down. A pretty woman with ratty hair
places a glass of whisky in front of me. The ice
cubes clink.

"So, Philip tells me that you're after some
help."

"Philip has told you correctly, yes. I would
have gone elsewhere, but I believe he was recently
killed by the Irish."

Straw hair looks at me hard. His eyes are
consumed with a mixture of curiosity and anger. I
have not been looked at like this for a
considerably long time. Not since the war, at
least.

"You *knew* Ronald?"

"I never knew him as Ronald, only as Mr
Barnard."

Straw hair nods, then relaxes and smiles.

"Ronald - your Mr Barnard to you - was my
brother. It's a pleasure to meet you. I'm Rufus."

Rufus holds out his hand and I shake it. I do
not miss a beat.

"Are you a Barnard also?"

"No, he picked the name because we both
used to go to Barnard Castle for our holidays
when we were kids. He bloody loved that place."

"Have you discovered why the Irish targeted
him?"

"Got no fucking clue mate, and I'm not going
to go up against them! Not the Irish. They're a
pack of animals. He was always into shady shit
that he would never tell me about. But that was
only fair, I would never tell him about my
business and if the truth be told, I couldn't trust
him as far as I could throw him. He probably got

mixed up in guns. How did you find him?"

"I knew Mr Barnard – excuse me – Ronald for over thirty years."

"He never once mentioned you."

"It's pleasing to hear that he was discreet, even to his own kin. We were good for each other. He hired me for a few jobs. Do you remember Gary the Geezer? 1972?"

"That was *you*?"

"Yes, at your brother's behest. I believe he was encroaching on turf."

Rufus takes a cigarette out from a crushed packet. The cigarette is bent and he straightens it before lighting it. He takes a few deep drags.

"That was *messy*. Okay, your credentials are sound. What are you after?"

"There is a man and his wife where I live, in a town called Effingham. Up the line a few hours in the Stour Valley. Are you aware of the place?"

"No, what have this couple done?"

"Their daughter was only thirteen and she hanged herself a couple of months back."

"Who is she to you?"

"She came to me for help. I tried, the father beat me up for my troubles, put me in hospital."

"Hence the stick?"

"Hence the stick."

"Why did she need your help?"

"The father was raping her. The mother let it happen."

Rufus takes in a sharp breath.

"Fucking hell."

"Fucking hell, indeed."

"So what do you want from me?"

I pull the King Edward coin out of my pocket.

"I'm going to sell this tomorrow to a coin collector. I'm guaranteed twenty-five thousand pounds for it. As soon as I do, I'll meet you wherever you like and hand the money over."

"And then?"

"And then I meet you in Effingham. You stage an invasion. I want the wife's throat slit instantly. The father, tie him up and leave him to me. Once I'm done, I'll need a lift back home."

"That's all? For twenty-five grand?"

"That's all. And when you're done, you'll have another twenty grand waiting for you."

He looks at me, trying to fathom my secrets. He gives up.

"Russell, I believe that you and I have a deal."

We shake hands. Another whisky is brought to us.

Sunlight streams in through the gap in the curtains. I wince. My head thumps, a dull ache. My mouth feels like cotton wool. My hip feels like it has been kicked by a donkey. I look around for my stick but it is not in my room. I walk uneasily through to the bathroom and look at myself in the mirror. The bags under my eyes could carry a month's worth of groceries. I have not shaved for several days. If I was to continue to grow a beard, I am sure that it would be pure white.

I get dressed silently and make my way down to have some breakfast. I see a familiar face, but do not know who it is, maybe a politician. I order four slices of toast with marmalade and a cafetiere of coffee.

I ask for a newspaper and am given it. It holds nothing of interest. There is a televised night planned for the murdered comedian. I shall make sure the television is switched off that evening.

I take a cab to Camden Passage, Islington, and hunt the antique shops for a cane. At my third stop, Grays Antiques, I find what I am looking for and pay fifty pounds for it.

TED

I AM SITTING in my 'comfy' chair. I have ingested amphetamine, which Rufus sorted out for me the evening I met him in the pub. I feel alert. I feel good. I look at the clock. It is two in the morning. Rufus says he will pick me up at three.

I make myself a cup of tea, try to focus on the night at hand, but I am bothered by a hallucination of Nicola. It appears that my mental malaise is back and is trying to talk me out of my course of action.

"You can't do this, not to my parents," Nicola says. She is sitting on my kitchen table. Her neck is black where the rope bit into it.

"There was a time I accepted all of these hallucinations as ghosts, as my punishments, but not any more," I say to her, to myself. "You do not exist. All you mean is that after all of this is over I need to go and see a doctor."

Nicola gets up and walks to the fridge and opens it. She sees nothing of interest and slams it shut.

"I'm so sorry, but you're not there. Why aren't you going away?" I say gently.

"You were supposed to help me."

"And now I'm avenging you. That's all I have."

Nicola looks sadly at me.

"What will Angela say when she discovers you've never had any marbles?"

"She won't"

"How are you going to be able to hide it?"

A car pulls up outside the house. I grab my cane and take a quick look in the mirror. I am all dressed in black. I have covered my cane in black electrical tape and muffled the tip so it does not make a noise when it connects with the ground. I close the door behind me, Nicola is no longer there. She does not follow. She is back in whatever part of my brain conjures her up.

"Rufus, good to see you."

Rufus looks at me, sees that I am high.

"Are you able to handle the drugs, old man?"

"Yes, they aren't an issue. It's either that or having me fall asleep on the job."

Rufus guffaws.

"Say hello to Jason and James in the back."

"Hello chaps." They both look to be in their thirties.

They both nod.

"They don't speak. They had their tongues cut out when they were kids."

"That's quite the something," I remark.

Rufus releases the handbrake and we drive off into the darkness, headlights off.

We pull up two streets from their house and walk towards it.

"What kind is it?"

"End of terrace," I answer.

"That's good."

James goes to the front of the house, Jason round the back. James brings out lock picking tools and makes quick work of the Yale. He nods at Rufus. Rufus takes out two balaclavas and throws one at me. He puts the other on, making sure it is in place. He then takes out a straight razor and enters the house. I follow him in.

We meet Jason at the bottom of the stairs. I

can only fathom that the back door was already unlocked for him to be able to get in so quickly. Jason gives him a torch which is covered in tape apart from a tiny hole that lets out a thin beam of light. Rufus creeps up the stairs as softly as a cat. He opens one of the doors, puts the torch in and looks back at us and nods. My heart trip-hammers. Rufus is swallowed by the blackness of the room. Jason follows him as does James.

I hear a slight cry and then something that sounds like torn fabric. A struggle.

Ted is in the kitchen, tied to his kitchen chair. I have not tied him in my preferred fashion in case Rufus has heard about how Robert was found. Ted's feet are tied to the front legs, his hands tied behind his back. He is gagged. I do not want him to talk to me.

Rufus comes into the kitchen. He holds the bloody straight razor. He wipes it on Ted's pyjama knee.

"Right, we'll be off now. Going to drive to the spot you suggested and we'll see you in what, half an hour?" Rufus asks.

"Yes. Can you please leave the razor?"

Rufus looks at Ted and laughs.

"I really do hope that you are going to remove his balls."

Ted tries to scream through his gag.

"I do believe that's what will end up happening."

"Nicola would have gone far, you know," I say to Ted. I am standing in front of him. "She was special, a rare breed. However, you and your dead wife up the stairs had to go and fuck her up.

Literally. She was a *child*. Wait there."

I leave him and go up the stairs and find Nicola's bedroom. There are pictures of New Order, Beastie Boys, The Housemartins and R.E.M. on the walls. By her bed there is a photograph of her sitting on a wall. She is smiling and looks happy. It is in a silver frame. I take the back off the frame and remove the photograph and put it in my back pocket.

I go back downstairs and walk straight to Ted and grab his balls. I squeeze them as hard as I can. He screams through the gag. I begin to slice his face, over and over and over. One slice takes his ear off. Another, his lip. I then cut deep into his testicles with the straight razor. Instantly his pyjamas are soaked red. Once his balls are free and dropped to the floor I work on his penis. My hands are covered in hot gushing blood. It is a remarkably easy task to remove his root. I go to the sink and grab a glass from the drainer. I catch a spurt of blood from his wounds. It takes thirty seconds for the glass to fill. Ted has slumped by this time. I take the glass of blood and the blade upstairs. The blade goes in his wife's hand and I pour the blood all over her offending hand and arm. Once finished I wash the glass in the bathroom sink.

Back in the kitchen I pull out my back-up blade and cut the ties that are holding Ted to the chair. He falls to the floor. I put the chair back neatly under the table even though it is soaked with blood. I then lift up his arms, one after the other and slash at them. I slice off a finger. Defensive wounds.

I take the can of petrol that James brought into the house, go upstairs and pour it all over Ted's dead wife, make my way downstairs and splash liberal amounts on Ted's body and make a trail into the lounge, over the sofa and to the front door. I turn off the kitchen light and the house is in complete darkness again.

Once at the door I take out a box of matches. I light one and then set fire to the box. It goes up in an urgent flurry of sulphur. I throw the box onto the petrol and it goes up, *whoomph*. I take my cane, close the door behind me and let the fire get on with its business.

"You really didn't have to do that you know," Nicola says as I walk away from the house, cutting through an alleyway on Kale Street.

"I did, otherwise you would have haunted me forever."

Rufus is waiting for me in the car.

"All good?"

"Yes. The house will be burnt to the ground soon enough."

"You really are a sort," he says.

"I'm not to be tempered."

"That I'm gathering. I wish I had talked to my brother about you, I'm sure he would have had some stories to tell."

I take off my clothes and put them in the bin bag that Rufus has provided. I get dressed into a pair of jogging bottoms, t-shirt and loafers.

"If anyone sees me in this, they'll know immediately that I've been up to something," I joke.

NEWS

I AM IN the shop. I have bought the *Stour Valley News* which is leading on the death of Ted and his wife for the third day in a row. The police are more than happy that it is a murder/suicide with the wife being the instigator. There are rumours that Ted's 'manhood' was hacked off. There are also rumours that she killed him because Ted was 'handsy' with his daughter.

I am happy.

The bell goes. It is Angela and Billy. Billy is in a wheelchair, his legs still in plaster.

"Why hello you two," I say, getting up easier than ever now. "How's the house settling in?"

"It's great. It's not haunted, like everyone says it is. This village can be a little too much at times."

"Don't I know it. And Billy, how are your legs feeling and are you here for a certain book?"

"They get very itchy under these plaster casts. And mum says that I'm not allowed to scratch them. Do you *really* have a copy of the sequel?"

I walk to the children's section and take out a hardback of *The Moon of Gomrath*.

"Here you go, the continuing adventures of Colin and Susan. This one is just as powerful and emotional as the first. Do you think you'll be able to handle it?"

"Yes, thanks ever so much, Mr Stickles."

"And do you think you'll be able to handle the price? I can't keep on giving you free books forever, you know!"

Billy looks up at his mum.

"How much?"

"Well, I would like to be invited around for dinner one day!"

Angela laughs.

"I think we can manage that."

As we are talking, the door opens. A man walks in. He is big, has difficulty breathing. He does so in big wheezy gulps.

"Hello, do . . . you . . . have . . . a . . . copy . . . of . . . *A Confederacy of Dunces*?" That he manages to say the title in one go is rather remarkable.

"I do, and I have a mint first edition, but I'm afraid I cannot let it go for anything less than one hundred pounds. It won the Pulitzer Prize for fiction, you know."

CHAPTER TWO

There were times when I was ordered to kill someone. It wasn't something I ever relished doing. I am not a psychopath. I repeat, the times when I had to, I was ordered to do so by my country. Does that make things worse or better? The honest answer is that I do not know.

There was a family man, a good man by all accounts, but he was a spy for the Germans. While I do not want to mention his name, he should be easy enough to look up. It was reported that he and his family were killed in a car crash outside their home, Millican.

I was told to deal with whoever was in the household with extreme prejudice. I didn't ask who was in the house, but I should have. I would have turned down the job.

I broke in quite easily and discovered that he was living there with his wife and two children, girls, both in their early teens. They all begged, but I had to do as I was told. I split them all into different rooms so they wouldn't see the other killed. I didn't put gags on them, we were in a house in the country, being heard wasn't an issue. I snapped the mother's neck first, then the girls. Quickly done.

I worked on the traitor last. I let him listen to his family's last moments. I asked him whether he regretted his choices. Regretted what side he was on.

He looked at me through his tears and told me that I would go to hell and that I would forever regret what I had done to his girls. All loyalty to his masters in Germany had vanished. Here was his price, paid in blood. The Reich could not protect him now. I told him that I was sure he was right, but I'd only be able to cross that bridge when I came to it.

I broke every single one of his ribs, punctured his lung in the process and stomped on both of his arms. Brought my foot down so hard on his back that I paralysed him from the waist down. These injuries were not enough to kill him. I was told not to kill him. He was to be left alive when the clean-up team put him in the car and arranged his crash. But I had to do the dirty work.

That night when I finally got home I went to bed and fell asleep straight away. No dreams, no nightmares. When I went to report to my bosses I did not protest about finding the girls in the slightest. And then I was given my next job and the girls were forgotten about.

I have not thought about those two girls until last week. They came crashing back into my subconscious forty-six years after I was ordered to kill them. And now I can't stop thinking about them. I should have let them go. But that would have made me the traitor. And the war was a many tentacled virus that was infinitely bigger than the budding offspring of someone who had no problem in selling out his fellow countrymen.

The girls now haunt my every waking hour and I don't know if I'll ever be able to stop them. They stand by me on either side as I sit writing this. They talk to me. They taunt me. Theirs are the remains that won't stay in their graves.

"I'm going to enjoy what I've got as long as it lasts."

—Patricia Highsmith,
The Talented Mr Ripley

A MAN AT WAR

(1941–1942)

"When you've learned that life
Is what you make it
Then you know the secret of it all"
—'Keep Smiling at Trouble'
Al Jolson and Buddy DeSylva

BUNKER

MY POSTCARD IS brief.

22.7.41

Mother, Stepfather,

All is well, London can be very challenging at times. Best foot forth, etc.

Russell

I miss Effingham. It is a very sleepy village. I miss the park, the moat, the woods. But most of all I miss the silence.

I reside in a bare room with a single bed and a table and chair at an address in London. I am not allowed to disclose this address to anyone, be it east, west, north or south. It is a secret address. To divulge this secret to anyone would be treason. I have a landlady who regards me with deep suspicion. I am sure she is responsible for the white feather under my door. I am not here to spy on the landlady, although if she gets in my way I have been told to kill her and staff will send in a replacement to take over her ownership. If I am to terminate her, *c'est la vie*. She would be nowhere near my first. I have no doubt repressed all of these swirling, abyssic deeds and thoughts until they will come spilling out of me in a shower of bile at a later date.

 Blackout. I make sure that there is no loose cardboard peeling away from the windows and I light a candle and get into bed. The old springs protest too much under my weight. I pull up my blankets and try to get comfortable. I look at the flame, it burns steady. My current book does not want to be read this evening. It is a book of ghost stories by M.R. James. I find my dreams are dangerous and loathsome if I read his tales before bed. I try to sleep. Bombs explode in the distance. It would be a blessing if I were to die in my sleep when I am old. But not now. Not like this. War is hazardous to one's health. I find it difficult.

I put on underpants, slacks, socks and make sure that my shoes are shined to military perfection. I follow with my shirt, plain cufflinks and tie. My blazer is slowly becoming threadbare at the elbows, I will have to sew some patches onto it.

I say goodbye to the impossibly mean landlady. She is hovering by the front door. There is no need for her to be so suspicious of me. My accent is perfectly English, she has seen and begrudgingly accepted my false papers which would pass any test as they were created by the finest forgers in England. However, the war has levelled everyone and we are all equally alien. We are told to only trust our loved ones. It's a sentiment with which I'd agree but I will be processing a file later on today about how a rather prominent politician is a spy for the Germans. His family will no doubt be thrilled with this turn of events once his past catches up with him.

I walk out onto the street; it's early, all is quiet. The air is still. I walk fast, noticing that four new houses have been destroyed. Smoke drifts from their remnants like the last wisps of a stubbed cigarette. There are children playing on the last site, climbing up the blasted brick, using the roof timbers as levers to hoist themselves up.

Shredded clothes and pages from books litter the street.

I catch the bus from my usual spot and try not to fixate on how ruined London is becoming. I think about a desolate future, what buildings could take their place if we lose the war. Germanic slave centres where we have to kowtow to Hitler each morning. I'd rather take my cyanide pill.

A girl sits across from me and she is trying her hardest not to give me a side glance. I turn and look at her. Directly. She has wavy hair and is wearing red lipstick. It appears that she may have rubbed some lipstick on her cheeks to make them glow. It gives them the look that one would find on a child's dolly. My view drifts out of the window. I wonder who she is. Trust no one.

I am not meant to jump off, but I depart from the bus as it slows down to take a corner; the girl is surprised by this sudden move. I nip down a side street. I turn right, right and right again. I am not followed. Maybe she simply liked the cut of my suit. I cannot be too careful. We are a country at war and I am a man at war.

I jump on another bus until I get to my destination. When I arrive I walk down a thin alleyway between two Victorian, but non-descript houses. These have both been reinforced to withstand direct hits. There is a tall black gate to the left. I open and close it behind me. There is a shed at the bottom of the small garden. I knock three times, pause and knock again. A shutter opens, a pair of flecked blue eyes stare hard at me.

"Juniper Trees are due a pruning," I say. The slide snaps shut and the door opens. I am confronted by a soldier in full military get-up. I walk down an incline, slowing slightly the further I descend. The temperature drops. I am glad that I put on a vest.

I walk for exactly six minutes and twenty-five seconds before I come to a steel door. I press a dirty white bell set into the concrete wall. I cannot hear it ring. Seconds later the door opens towards me. This I always forget and have to take a hurried and apologetic step backwards.

This time it is a woman at the other side of the door, her hair is in the current fashion and she is wearing a light brown uniform that denotes her as a Lance-Corporal.

"Stickles, Russell, 69666," I say, standing to attention. I hate that I instinctively do this.

She nods silently and lets me pass. I am now in the main hub and beyond me are hundreds of tables, fully lined with women on phones, typing, decoding this, that and the other. The noise in this cavern is like the chatter of a million magpies. I walk as fast as I can to the other side of the hall, to another set of winding corridors, to the relative quiet of offices, meeting and break rooms. I am not noticed. I am normally unnoticeable,which made today's happenstance on the bus all the more unusual.

I make my way to room 636, knock and a voice from within barks "enter!".

"Stickles, sit down, there's a good chap," Wing Commander Dennis Wheatley points to a chair opposite his. He takes a final drag on his cigarette and stubs it out violently into the heavy ashtray that's placed precariously atop a pile of folders, paperwork and other miscellaneous ephemera. He moves the ashtray back onto the middle of the pile, aware that it could tip over. He is not wearing a jacket; that is hung up on a coat stand. His sleeves are rolled to above the elbows and there are sweat patches under both arms of his white cotton shirt that have insidiously soaked the fabric to almost his nipples. It is not an alluring sight, but Dennis does not care. There is a map of some county on the wall with several pins in it. I cough, the smoke chastising my lungs.

"Right, let's get you up to speed, shall we? Oliver Stanley has had to leave, his wife is terminally ill. We're expecting John Bevan to come in and take control at some point, but when, we don't know. Everything is running as normal, so there is no need to worry."

"That's a shame about Lady Maureen," I say, my tone neutral.

Wheatley doesn't respond.

"We tried to set up a honey-trap for your man," he says, changing the subject to current matters. "Surprisingly, he didn't take the bait. We're of a thinking that he may be a homosexual. Do you indulge?"

"Excuse me?"

"Buggery. Do you indulge in buggery? You won't be judged by me, and it'll be between us, of course."

"No." The word hangs between us. I hope he catches the firmness in my voice.

"Hmm. That's a shame. We might have snared him that way." Wheatley rifles through papers on his desk and passes me a vanilla file.

"Read that, it's his daily habit. Spends a bit of time in the park, feeds some ducks. His local was the Speared Boar until it was bombed Friday last, now it's the Hooked Carp on Morning Street. He's there most lunches. You, Stickles, have to really step up your game. Try and talk to him before you both retire to your rooms. It feels like we're paying you to simply exist at the moment."

"Yes. Understood."

Wheatley looks up, sees my face and grins. "Don't worry chap, you'll see some action soon. Once this is wrapped up there's a job I'd like you to take a look at in your neck of the woods. Effingham, isn't it?"

"Yes."

"It'll be an interesting one." He doesn't tell me any more. Instead he opens a drawer and reaches in, pulling out a thick book with an orange cover and a horse on it. "Here's a copy of my fifth, *The Devil Rides Out*. I know you talked about wanting to read it back when we first met. You needn't try to search any more, I found a spare copy in the attic."

"This is extremely generous of you. Thank you ever so much, Sir." I take the book and open it. He has dedicated it.

For Russell Stickles,

The book that brought me more fan mail than any other to date.

From Dennis Wheatley, Aug '41

It is a strange dedication, but I thank him once more and I am dismissed. I make my way to one of the mess rooms, again, incredibly smoky, and pour myself a cup of extremely bitter coffee. I sit in the corner and sip gently, mulling over in my mind Wheatley's veiled warning. I clearly have to be more proactive. It is, however, quite difficult to spy on someone who lives their life in their room and leaves at odd times, hence the external teams having to tail and follow his movements.

My coffee remains half-drunk. I abhor leaving a mess, but the smoky atmosphere gets to me.

RAID

I WAKE WITH a start. The noise of sirens fills the room, consumes my heart and lungs, makes my body vibrate. I grab my spectacles from the cabinet, my torch from the top drawer and put on my dressing gown and slippers. I meet him on the landing and hold out my arm as a gesture for him to go first. He smiles briefly, nods and then quickly makes his way down the squeaky staircase. I follow close behind. He is wearing scent. It has a hint of raspberry to it.

The landlady is waiting by the back door, smoking a cigarette and her hair is full of cheap rollers, all held together by a hastily fashioned wrap of fabric, possibly part of an old curtain.

A tremendous shock runs through us as a bomb hits a house at the end of the street. The sky lights up, we hear screams. We run to the bottom of the garden and into the Anderson shelter. I turn on the torch. He has his, as does a youngish girl of around twenty with cherub-like features. She sits on the bench gently crying. The landlady slams the door shut behind us as a massive blast threatens to end the world. The air is sucked out from the shelter, the heat tears through the gaps in the doors and I am flung back, crashing into the girl. My torch hits the roof of the shelter, and I bang my head against something hard.

My mouth is full of dust. I cough, my lungs don't feel as if they want to work. I panic and try to take a deep breath. Something presses down on me. I free my right hand from sharp rubble and with as much strength as I can muster, push whatever it is away from me.

I get to my knees. It seems as if there is fire all around me. One side of the Anderson's doors have been blasted inwards. I crawl outside onto the wet grass. Darkness teases me.

The landlady's house looks as if it has been cleaved in half. Smoke billows out from the roof in thick, urgent plumes. I see a shadow scrabbling up felled masonry, trying to get to a room that looks like a showroom. The wall is missing.

I cough. I rasp. I wheeze. I keep my body as close as I can to the wet grass. It is then I realise that I am naked. My clothes have been blasted from me. The heat of my skin is punishing. I see him come back down, jumping from one room to the other, a massive rip taken from the flooring. He stabilises and vanishes into the darkness. I do not hear him scream.

A horrendous *whooshing* fills my ears, it takes at least thirty seconds to realise it is, in fact, the sound of my heartbeat. I make my way slowly, so slowly up the debris and into the mouth of hell. I see a torn section of sheet, maybe a tablecloth. I wrap it around my face. I yell as I put my hand down on something sharp. I lift my hand slowly to my face. There is a long, ugly nail, twisted and red hot protruding from my palm. I grab the head with my fingers and rip it out. The heat from the nail cauterizes the wound.

From the inferno, amazingly he stumbles out, his arms full. He does not see me crouching.

"*Was ist das?*" I yell. I am unsure if he hears me. I slowly get to my feet, trying to stop my body from violently lurching. I place my injured   hand on his shoulder. He stops. I scream as I bring down the chunk of masonry that's in my other hand. His head is cracked as easily as an eggshell. A spray of blood hits me in the face. He falls down to his knees, his arms dropping his secrets. A small transmitting radio and a book. I let the stone fall to the grass. I pick up the transmitter and book and make my way to the back of the garden, to the destroyed shelter, to the waiting corpses of the crying girl and the suspicious landlady, suspicious no more.

I slowly weave in and out of consciousness like a spider building its web. Numinous dark shadows swarm around me, ready to drag me to hell.

"We've got you," a disembodied voice shouts at me in a cockney accent. It makes perfect sense that the Devil's spawn are all from East London. I am lifted to my feet and dragged away from the direct hit, my hands grasping for dear life onto the spy's wares.

I am taken to the Red Dennis where I am given a blanket to cover my modesty. I am left alone as the firemen tackle the blaze.

"How are you feeling?"

I look up. A kindly face, a face covered in soot apart from around his eyes, which he constantly wipes at with a damp cloth.

"Like death. I need to get to a phone box."

"You'll be lucky," the fireman chuckles, his voice soft. "Main exchange was taken out tonight. Will take days to fix. Do you have any clothes?"

I shake my head, no.

"There's a fire station only five minutes walk away. Straight on, left at the end of the street and over the Whipping Bridge. You know it?"

"Yes."

"Tell them that William Sansom sent you. They'll kit you out with some clothes. Tell them to take some money out of the biscuit tin in the kitchen, and I'll pay it back. Can you remember my name?"

"Sansom. William Sansom."

He smiles again and looks around his blasted surroundings. He grows in stature, the king of taming these destroyed buildings and half says to himself as I get up to leave, "this will make one hell of a book some day."

"William?"

He turns to me. "Yes?"

"I rather think I need an ambulance."

Darkness.

BURNED

I WAKE TO the sound of a piano playing. I am unsure if it is a real piano or a recording of one. I cannot sense any vibrato. I lie as still as I can, my eyes closed. The pain begins as little needles, millions of little needles, skitter over my chest. I am propped up on pillows but as I try to sit up tight sheets hold me down. My hands are restricted. I crack open one eyelid. My hands are red raw. I am handcuffed.

There is a policeman sitting at the end of the bed. He is not wearing his helmet, that is placed on the floor beside him. He has red hair and a small snub nose that looks out of place on his face. It makes him look like a rodent one would keep as a pet.

The pain really hits home now and I want to wail, but that is not my way. It feels like a burning meteor has been placed on my chest. The policeman sees that I am awake. He stands up and looks around, helpless.

A Matron appears, doughy face, streaks of silver in her hair disappearing into the stiff, starched cap she has perfectly placed on her head.

"Take this." She puts a pill on my tongue and makes me drink it down with a sip of tepid water. That opens me up and I try to get her to indulge me with more fluids.

"No. You'll throw up."

"Who are you?"

I open my eyes to a man, small, wearing a dark blue blazer. He is standing by me. Lower ministry job. His face betrays no emotion.

"I cannot tell you."

His face beams. He thinks he has a spy on his hands.

"You were found with some very interesting paraphernalia on you. We're waiting for someone to come and analyse it. You're going to hang."

My mind scrambles for the protocol.

"Phone Knightsbridge 735. When you are asked why you are calling, say that there is an injured falcon. 69666. Give them our location. Then sit back and have a cup of tea."

His face darkens.

"I won't be hanging this time, whoever you are, you petty little thing," I sigh, as a comforting blanket of pain relief decides it's time to give me a cuddle. "And please remove these handcuffs. You won't want me in them."

I close my eyes again.

"Who *are* you?" he asks again, his voice lacking his previous confidence and conviction.

"To *you*? I'm *nobody*."

The small man nods to the policeman, a different one this time, short cropped hair and a monobrow, steps forward and uncuffs my hands from the rails that run on either side of the bed.

"Only until I make the call. If you've tried to pull a fast one, the cuffs go back on," the small man says, nervously.

"Very fair." I grimace as an unexpected creep of pain constricts my chest.

"Hello Russell."

I open my eyes.

A female, early 40s, hair carefully pinned back, wearing an orange two-piece utility suit. Not professional, but welcoming.

"Hello."

"I'm Mrs McGuinness. You can call me Doreen."

"Hello Doreen." I struggle to sit up.

"I've been sent by the Controlling Station. I'm going to be taking down your statement. Take your time, try and remember everything you can."

"Of course."

"What have the doctors said about your injuries?"

"These," I lift up my hands, "in time will be fine, the nail that went through my hand was so hot it killed off any chance of it being infected, which is nice," I chuckle. "My chest and stomach will sadly be a road map of scars for the rest of my life. But I got off luckily."

Doreen nods, sympathetically. "I drove past this morning on my way here. You were very lucky to survive. Looks like it was two bombs, one landed directly on top of the other. An extremely uncommon occurrence."

"Anything left?"

"The rest of the house has collapsed. Your room was completely obliterated, so we weren't able to rescue anything for you. I've left a fresh change of clothes with the Matron and some money to get you to control when you're discharged."

"Thank you." I breathe in, wincing.

"So. Tell me what happened."

"You didn't kill him, you know," Doreen states, looking at me. My heart sinks.

"Really? I thought I came down pretty hard."

"You did. He's in a coma, has been operated on. The transmitter is an interesting piece of kit, the technical chaps have been having a field day with it. The book however, is remarkable."

"What does it contain?"

"We don't know yet."

"Excuse me?" I asked, puzzled.

"It's in code. Not German. We've sent it off to try and crack it."

"Baker Street?"

Doreen raises an eyebrow. "You've kept your ear to the ground."

"Controlling can be a hard place to keep a secret."

Doreen guffaws at this, her face lights up. She is not unattractive.

"Yes, very true." She sighs, rubs her right eye with the palm of her hand.

"What will happen to him if he wakes?"

"Depends on the damage you did. If he wakes up with a headache, he'll be interrogated. If the codex hasn't been cracked he'll be asked about it. Then he'll be either turned against the Germans or hanged. I suspect the latter. No great loss."

"No great loss," I agree.

Doreen stands up, places her notepad on the chair and brushes her skirt down. She picks the pad up, places it in her bag and holds out her hand.

"It's been a pleasure meeting you, Mr Stickles."

"Likewise." I take her hand gently, so as not to hurt mine.

RECOVERY

THE NURSE FINISHES bandaging me then helps me on with my shirt. It's green, not a colour I feel comfortable wearing, but I dress without complaint. I put on a pair of slacks, brown socks and smart leather shoes. The jacket is tight around the middle, but that's more to do with the bandages than an expanding paunch. Give me ten years of good living as soon as war is over. I put the envelope containing five pounds in my inside pocket, thank the nurse and the Matron who has come to see me off. I leave the hospital, I turn right at the gate and I find that I am on Chapel Road. There are three houses gone on this street, but the trees, all poplars, remain. Children play together in small clusters. One of them, a little girl, stares at me as I walk past. I wave at her. She smiles, revealing three missing teeth.

My shoes pinch. They have yet to be broken in. My grand idea of walking to Controlling Station is turning into a rather stupid one. The leather rubs against the thin material of my socks. I decided to take the shoes off and I throw them into the remnants of someone's house. My feet instantly thank me and I walk carefully, remembering how I spent my childhood running around with bare feet. It didn't hurt me then and it won't hurt me now.

A woman pushing a pram bids me a good afternoon. I stand to one side to let her past. She glances down at my feet, for why I have no idea, but once she sees that I am not wearing shoes, she hurries, pushing her pram quickly. I chuckle to myself, shaking my head. I spy a telephone at the end of the road and decide to phone Mother and Stepfather and tell them what's happened. They have not heard from me for a couple of weeks and I forbade Controlling to inform them that I was in hospital. It would have caused too many questions to be asked and I didn't want Mother upset.

The switchboard operator asks me to whom I would like to speak. I ask for Effingham 691. My mother is only one of seven households to have a phone in the village. I don't think I'll ever have a phone myself. I do not like the thought of anyone being able to get a hold of you any time they like.

There is no answer. I regretfully hang up and see a bus turn the corner, getting ready to stop. I run for it then pull up short, wincing in pain as a sharp stone cuts through the ersatz fabric of my sock and into the flesh of my foot. The bus pulls away and I stand there, dejected. My foot throbs. After a minute I gather myself and limp the three and a half miles to Controlling.

"Why on earth didn't you phone and ask for a car to come and pick you up?" Wheatley asks, his face puzzled.

"I don't know really, I didn't want to be a nuisance."

Wheatley offers me a cigarette, I shake my head, *no*. He takes one for himself, taps it on the table and puts it in his mouth, lighting it with a heavy chrome and bakelite desk lighter, shaped like a rocket or missile. He puffs away, getting maximum smoke into his lungs and relaxes back into his seat and exhales.

"You're an odd fish, Stickles. You know that, don't you?"

"Yes sir. Odd. But doesn't that make me suited for where we find ourselves?"

Wheatley chuckles and flicks ash into the ashtray.

"You're right. Remarkable times call for remarkable men. I've never met anyone like you though. You might even make it into one of my books one day. I take it the book I gave you didn't survive. No matter, will source you another."

"Blown up, I'm afraid. Another copy would be lovely, thank you. I'd rather you didn't put me in a book, Sir. I wouldn't want Mother shocked. She's a fan of your work."

Wheatley steals a sly glance to see if I'm joking or not.

"You're being put up in a hotel for the next couple of weeks so you can get your strength back. We could send you to Effingham to recuperate, but if we need you in a hurry and the train lines are down, it'll be a problem."

"What about the 'interesting situation' you had in Effingham?"

"Not for a while yet. MI5 are still titting about."

Wheatley opens a drawer and pulls out an envelope stuffed with money. "This should get you a full wardrobe and any other things you might have lost. No need to pay for the hotel, we've taken over the running of it. There's a doctor on site who'll be around if you need him and they have a much better bunker than the one you nearly found yourself blown up in."

"Gas mask?"

"No need to pick up one of those. Incidentally, if you had been wearing one, it would have fused to your face. It did your landlady."

"The war is giving us so many pleasing images that will keep us company in our dotage," I say, sarcastically, but without malice.

"Quite." We both fall silent.

"Stickles, there's a job I want you to do," Wheatley says quietly, sliding a photograph across the table to me.

I pick it up and look at it. A female. Pretty.

"Captured or free-floating?"

"Picked up yesterday. She was out during curfew, which isn't frowned upon, really – but the warden asked to see her papers and as luck would have it he just got a bad feeling about her and arrested her right there on the spot."

"She didn't try to get away?"

"Yes, she did, but he threw his torch at her and it bounced off her head. Good night."

"Tell me about her."

"As far as we can tell she's been in the country since '38, buried herself down deep. We did the same before War was declared, sent a couple of agents over there. Of the five we sent, two are still over there, unmolested, one dead. The other two we had to bring back as their cover was blown."

"Has she managed to divulge anything major?"

"One operational manual regarding the development of a new rocket, that's the big one that we think she's responsible for. She was caught, as I said, outside curfew with a couple of pages on her person. Transpires that she was sleeping with the boss of the factory, of course."

"Of course? Not *everyone* gets that close. Don't dismiss her through the use of her sex," I say.

Wheatley grunts.

"Don't be a damned fool. She's a spy. Of course she's going to try and sleep with the enemy. That's why *we* breed them. To worm their way in. They are parasites. Being parasitic is what they do."

"Very well. I accept everything that you have to say. I will go at her. I'll be like the troops at Ypres. I'll go for the eye."

Wheatley does not know what I am going on about.

"Don't be so bloody odd and mysterious. I just want you to break her. Make her feel that whatever she has faced from us so far is nothing, a blip, a stone being skipped across the river."

"You've had a good go at her?"

"For a while. Everyone's having a pop at her. She's become sport."

Wheatley stands up and turns to the wall. I slide my hand across the table and take his fountain pen that is sneaking its tip out from under a pile of papers. I put it into my pocket as he turns round.

"Do you think you can break her?"

I get up, wincing in pain. Wheatley immediately comes to my side.

"I'll walk out with you," he says.

THE STORM

I AM TAKEN to her cell. I wait patiently while a very tall soldier fumbles with the heavy key in the lock. Once open the door swings inwards. This is so any prisoner has to step back and cannot use the door for leverage.

Bettina sits on the floor. Her bed is neatly made. She is wearing a dirty white shirt and slacks. Her hair is mousy. She does not look at me when I come in. I stand in the middle of the cell. The tall soldier reappears with a chair for me to sit on.

"Hello." I say, crossing my legs. I reach into my pocket and pull out a packet of cigarettes and a box of matches. I throw them, they land at her dirty feet.

"My name is Mr Stickles. You can call me Russell. I'm here to get information out of you. It appears that you have been very busy with several members of our Government. And others." I pause. She has not moved.

"In fact, you might have never been caught if it wasn't for a fellow compatriot of yours, a chap called Peter Wolf."

A flicker of her eyelids.

"Peter had a little book. It was in code and was rather hard to crack. But crack it we did," I lie. "And your name pops up on more than one occasion. Peter, well, he's dead now. Shot yesterday morning about a mile from here. Not a dignified death in the least. Crying. Didn't even give a *sieg heil*." Another lie. Lying is always fun.

Bettina looks at me and reaches for the cigarettes and matches. She removes one and lights it, taking small, stuttery puffs. It makes her cough.

"Your first for a while? Relish it."

"So, what do you want from me, Mr Stickles?" Bettina says, her accent sounding so English as to be perfect. "Do you want me to give up all of my secrets?" Her accent changes to her native German. "It will never happen. What I have stays in here." She taps the side of her head with her finger. "And you'll never be able to get it out."

I smile.

"That's why I'm here, Bettina, and not some lower-functioning MI19 fool who'd threaten you with the firing squad or persuade you to try and turn against your handlers. I knew within seconds of coming in here that you're more than happy to assume martyr status."

"Look at you. You are *nothing*. Do you really think you can scare me?" Bettina laughs. She stands up now, leaning back against the wall. The tall soldier, hired I am sure more for his size than his brains, steps into the cell, I hold my hand up, *no further.*

"Yes. Look at *me*. You will become more familiar with my face than that of your own father." I stand up abruptly, swallowing the pain I feel. Bettina does not flinch. This is good. She will be enjoyable.

"I'll be here tomorrow morning at eight sharp. Make sure you've not had anything to eat, because your breakfast will be the first thing to go and I don't want vomit on my shoes. Good evening."

I pick the chair up and leave the cell. The soldier closes the door behind me. I place the chair down and slowly make my way up the winding stone staircase and back to the office where Archie Kier is waiting for me. He is smoking a pipe.

"How did she take you?"

"I've certainly given her enough to make sure of a sleepless night. Now, I need someone to go into her cell, remove all of her bedding and strip her down to her knickers."

Archie sits up straight.

"Really?"

"Yes. Immediately. I don't want to give her an option of taking the easy way out. And first thing tomorrow, 5am, I want her delivered to the Cage. She can wear a shirt with the sleeves cut off and her underwear."

Archie shouts. "Staff!"

The soldier who had opened the cell door for me arrives and Archie gives him his orders. The soldier gives me a queer look on his way out.

"Fancy a drink?"

I don't, but a change of scenery would be good.

"Where were you thinking?"

"Ah, nowhere fancy, just a small pub called the Argosy not too far away from here, used by a number of us. However, once all this mess is over and done with I have a place I go to. One of the best and most secretive little clubs in London."

"Do carry on." I say, brow raised in interest.

"It doesn't have a name and I'm not sure it officially exists. I'll try and get you in. But not tonight."

We are in the Argosy. All of the windows have been boarded up and heavy curtains closed over them. I drink whisky by candlelight. The taste soothes me and I think about what the morning will bring. I am not too arrogant to think that I will break her by lunch. She has the mindset of a person who lives minute by minute. Another minute survived is another minute she is alive. As the hustle and bustle of the pub continues around me I close my eyes. I imagine that I am sitting in a chair. I am tied to it. My hands strain against the rough hemp. My wrists are bloody. A light is shone in my eyes. It is so bright that it bursts into my mind even when my eyes are closed as tight as they can be. I am barked at. I am screamed at. I am cajoled. I am pleaded with. I am threatened. I am struck. I have a gun rammed down my throat, it tears soft flesh. It will make swallowing difficult. I have fingernails removed. I have a hammer taken to my toes. My thigh is stabbed with a knife. My fingers are broken. My teeth are removed with a pair of rusty pliers. I smile through blood. I have my hands thrust into burning sand. Boiling sugar is thrown at my bare genitals.

"Another drink, Russell?"

I open my eyes. Archie Kier looks at me quizzically.

"Asleep? Already?"

"No, no," I say. "Just imagining what would happen if the roles were reversed. If I was the caught spy."

Archie looks stunned for a second. He genuinely doesn't know how to reply. He pauses, thinks some more and says truthfully, "If you were a spy, I don't think anything could get you to speak. And God help England if you were. You'd be our greatest enemy."

"Thank you for the compliment. And yes, another whisky will be grand."

DAY ONE

I AWAKE IN sheer panic. I fall out of bed heavily, lurch to my feet and stagger to the bathroom where I draw myself a glass of cold water from the bathroom sink. I gulp deeply, then explode into a coughing fit as it goes down the wrong hole. I fall to my knees, the tiles of the bathroom cold. I cough and cough and cough.

At some point it subsides. I carefully stand, using the sink to balance myself and I look in the mirror. I have bags under my eyes. My head does not feel too fuzzy. Archie tried his best to fill me with more alcohol, but I reminded him of the importance of the task at hand and he understood and drank my share.

I run a cold bath and get in. The extreme temperature shocks my system. Soothes my healing scars. I am instantly awake, instantly ready. I dry myself, patting my burns and wrap around fresh bandages and get dressed. Fresh pants, fresh socks. I do not wear a tie today because Bettina will have her hands free during some parts of her experience and I do not want to be throttled by her.

I eat kippers in milk for breakfast and chase it down with a gallon of sweet tea. Doctor Gentle, as he has been nick-named by everyone, nods at me as he walks past to get his food. I idly wonder what nickname I have been given, then stop. It would no doubt upset me if I heard it.

I am waiting outside the hotel for the car. A female is my chauffeur. She gets out and opens the door for me. I hand her my briefcase and duck in. She tries to speak to me on our journey to the

Cage. I ignore her, and concentrate on what will be a very long day ahead.

My driver does not smile when she opens the door.

"Kensington Palace Gardens, sir." She hands me my briefcase.

"Thank you. At ease." I give her the command knowing I have no power to.

I walk up the long drive until I am at the mansion. Lieutenant Colonel Scotland is waiting for me.

"You know we could do this ourselves, Stickles," he remarks haughtily. His tie is slightly askew.

"Not this one. She would give you the runaround for weeks."

"She'd soon give up her secrets. Pull out her fingernails. That'll have her singing from the rafters."

I sigh and stop dead. Scotland looks at me, his round spectacles irritate me.

"They've tried starving her. They've tried to freeze her, they've tried making her too hot. She's had 'In the Mood' played over and over again, blaring into her cell. The soldier tasked with that job ended up shooting himself because he couldn't bear hearing it one more time. Bettina Jarzinck is not your normal spy. She's hardened steel. Direct hits do not break her."

"And you will?"

I smile thinly.

"I will. Today is Tuesday. She'll be broken by Saturday."

Scotland chuckles.

"Very well Stickles, are you willing to place a bet?"

"I do not bet. But if I succeed, you have to send one hundred pounds to her family."

"What?" Scotland erupts into an apoplexy of confusion and anger.

"Anonymously, if you wish."

"One more question," Scotland reaches out and holds onto my arm. "Why here and not Camp Twenty?"

"I cannot *abide* 'Tin Eye' Stephens. He's half-German. Relishes in going after his own kind."

"The man's also half-English. The better half of him."

"So says you."

I enter the mansion.

I am sitting at a desk. My briefcase is in front of me. My briefcase is empty, but Bettina will not know that.

She is brought in cuffed. I look appreciatively at her legs. I ask the guard to uncuff her. He protests. I repeat my order. Bettina's arms are heavily bruised. She also has a fresh mark on her face.

"Who did that to you?" I ask.

"What are you going to do, reprimand them?" she says gently.

I shrug my shoulders in defeat. She has a point.

"There is a man I despise," I carry on, "His name is Stephens. He says, and excuse me if I don't remember correctly: "'Never strike a prisoner. It is an act of cowardice. In the second place, it is not intelligent. A prisoner will lie to avoid further punishment and everything he says thereafter will be based on a false premise.'" I can promise you now Bettina that I will not strike you.

But I have to disagree about the prisoner lying to you. This can be avoided if you have controls in place. Which we have."

"Do you have a cigarette?"

"No. Only this salt."

I reach into my pocket and bring out a largish salt cellar that I took from the mess room. I place it next to me. I put the briefcase on the floor.

"Guard!" I yell.

The guard enters and I beckon him to stand behind Bettina.

"If she tries to look away from me, reposition her head. If she closes her eyes for more than a few seconds, I will tell you to forcefully open them. You will never hit her. Understood?"

"Yes sir."

"Good." I begin to stare at Bettina.

"I need to use the toilet, please."

"You have a perfectly good seat to urinate on if you so desire."

"Head."

"Head."

"Head."

"Head."

"Head."

"Eyes."

"Head."

"Change of guard!"

"Head."

"Eyes."

I look at my watch. 4pm. It has been eight hours. This is enough.

"Guard, tilt her head back."

I get up, my left knee pops. I pick up the salt and in a flash am around the other side of the table and press my hand down on the supraorbital ridge, pulling up the top eyelid. I see the remnants of old mascara, or as we like to call it, the 'miracle eye-liner'. Her face has not been washed since she was captured.

I sigh.

I pour a liberal helping of salt directly into Bettina's open eye. She screams and tries to move her head.

"Guard, firm."

I move to her other eye.

"That's enough, you can let go."

Bettina collapses onto the floor, desperately trying to get the salt out of her eyes.

"Rubbing will only make it worse," I advise.

I put the cellar back in my pocket. I pick up my briefcase.

"Till tomorrow," I open the door and close it firmly behind me.

I am about to leave when Scotland collars me.

"What nonsense was that?" he chides.

"Take her back, please. Thank you for your time."

I walk through the grounds and to the waiting car. I have another driver.

"Where to, sir?"

"The hotel, please."

DAY THREE

"EYES."
    "HEAD."
    "HEAD."
    "Head."
    "Head."
    "Head."
    "Head."
    "Head."
    "Eyes."
    "Head."
    "Head."
    "Eyes."
    "Eyes."
    "Eyes. Wipe those smears from your fingers."
    "Head."
    "Head."
    "Eyes."

"Right. Time for a spot of lunch. Soldier, can you organise it? A simple salad each will be fine." The tall soldier lets go of holding Bettina's swollen head.

"You can rest on the table for a moment or two, that's fine," I motion to her. She obliges.

The door opens and the guard comes in with two finely-prepared salads. He places them down in front of us. Bettina is not given a fork or knife.

"Head."

The guard holds her head and I pick up the salt. She gives out a scream of fright. I lightly dust salt over my tomatoes.

"Let go."

The guard lets go.

187

"Eat, Bettina."

She picks up a tomato and places it in her mouth.

"Salt?" I offer.

She visibly shrinks back.

I eat my salad in silence. She watches me through heavily crusted eyes.

DAY FIVE

"GOOD MORNING!" I say extra cheerfully as I enter Bettina's cell. She is lying on her bed in nothing but her underwear.

"Now, I'm going to be quick, I'll take you back to when we met at that posh mansion. I don't know if you saw anything of it other than our room, were you blindfolded at the time? Never mind, I said something about not striking you, and believe me, I've wrestled with that all week because you are a very tough girl. However, a promise is a promise. Guard!"

Bettina sits up to attention as the tall soldier enters the cell.

"Hold her, make sure she doesn't squirm."

"What are you going to do to me?" she says, her voice cracking. The guard picks her up and puts his arms through hers, effectively pinning her arms behind her back.

I pull out my wallet from my inside pocket and from it withdraw a curved veterinary needle with fine thread hanging from it. I step towards her and show her it.

"Bettina, I could look at you for much longer, you *are* easy on the eye, even for a *German*. However, I'm sure that you're more than sick of looking at *me*. I've decided therefore, that it'll be best if I sew your eyelids shut. I *will* try to not pop your eyeballs as I do it, but I can't promise."

Bettina breaks.

I dash off a quick letter to Scotland.

As of 10am this morning, Bettina has given a full and true account of her time in this country. We have five more names to go after. I believe she'll be shot early Sunday morning before the local vicar holds his service. I'm sure it's fine for you to wait till after War is over to send her next of kin the proceeds of our wager. Burn this letter.

Cordially yours,

R. Stickles.

I am feeling very proud of myself.

THE CLUB

IT IS MONDAY. I do not want to go into work. Wheatley, I am informed, has been moved to another part of the country due to a more than credible threat to his life. Archie Kier is waiting for me in an office down another corridor. He is unkempt and should really run a comb through his hair.

"Bloody hell Stickles, you're a wonder!" He gets up from his chair and comes to shake my hand. I am appalled, but say nothing. I do not want to take any delight from my victory.

"Were you there?" I ask.

"Yes. She was brought out. Asked for a cigarette, took two puffs and flicked it at the soldiers who were there to put her down. Chuckled as the hood was put on her head. She was asked if she had any last words."

"And did she?"

Archie looks at me thoughtfully before answering.

"Yes, she did. For you."

"Really? What were they?"

"Russell Stickles needs to lose his virginity."

My next words stick in my throat. My vision swims for only a second.

"She really said that?"

"Yes, and everyone laughed, even though most of the people there didn't know who you were."

"Did you?"

"Did I what?"

"Did you laugh?"

"Of *course* I did. It was *funny*."

I smile, knowing there will be ample time for Archie to meet an unexpected end.

"Well," I say, "it *is* funny. What a way to go out."

"Bravest person I've ever seen. Almost cantered to the post they tied her to. Died instantly, clean heart shot and that saucy little Kraut was cremated by lunch."

I think about Bettina's legs and small dirty feet. They way they seemed to float across the stone floor like a ballerina practising before a show. I think about untying her from the post that her body is slumped against. I take her back to the cell and wash her feet until they are clean.

I snap out of my daydream.

"So what's next?"

"You go home."

"I do?"

"Yes. Tomorrow you go back to Effingham. You'll be contacted when you're there. Who by, I don't know, but they'll use the proper codes. Do you need a place rented for you or can you go back and stay with your family?"

"I'd prefer a rented place for the short term. I don't want my mother finding out about my scars – these will be bad enough to talk to her about." I lift up my hands, they are still an angry red.

"You'll be met off the train by someone who will take you to your new lodgings. But before you go, I said I'd take you to the strange club I belong to. You certainly fit the one part of the criteria now."

"And what's that, pray I ask?"

"You're responsible for the death of a spy. Instant membership."

We descend the stairs and turn left into a circular room. The walls are lined with books. We approach the bar. There is a stocky man with mutton chop sideburns and a scar that runs down the side of his face.

"I have someone I'd like to bring in as a member," Archie says.

"Has he?"

"Yes."

"Write your name, date of birth and an address that we can post something to on this bit of paper here," the man says.

I raise an eyebrow. "I do hope that this information won't be for sale to the highest bidder."

The man growls. "Who do you fucking take me for?"

"Russell!" Archie hisses. "Just write it down. Don't show me up."

"Can I use Controlling as my temporary address?"

"Yes."

I do as I'm told.

"First year is free. Next year there will be a fee of £10. It'll go up one pound for every year you're a member here. You'll be given your own password that only you'll have. That'll be posted out to you in due course. It'll then change every six months. We have the right to revoke your membership at any time without having to give a reason. Do you understand?"

"Yes. Certainly."

"Then welcome," mutton chops says with a rather lovely smile. "First drink is on the house. What will it be?"

"Do you have anything non-alcoholic?"

"No."

"Then I'll have a scotch."

"Are you sure I'll be able to take a book back to Effingham with me?"

"Of course," Archie replies.

I scan the wall of books.

"Do you think it would be fine if I took *Grapes of Wrath*?"

"Fine," mutton chops barks.

I stand up, take the hardback and look at it.

"Thank you very much, I'll take good care of it."

"You better."

I down my scotch.

"Another?" I ask Archie.

We stagger back. Around us the sirens begin to wail. We giggle at each other. I trip, sprawling onto the pavement. I cannot move. I howl with laughter.

"You . . . have . . . to . . . get . . . up!" Archie says, weaving back and forth as he tries to pull me up.

"Leave me be!" I shout at him. "I'm fine here, I just want to *sleeep*."

"You really are a beast, Stickles," Archie says and he staggers away from me. I hear him whistling as he meanders up the road. I put my head back down on the cold pavement. I believe that it might sober me up somewhat.

"Till tomorrow you..."

A deadly whistling noise from up above. I put my hands over my head. For the second time it feels like the earth is being torn apart. I feel hot air rushing over me. If I could I'd burrow my head into the road. Heavy lumps of stone rain down on me. I am injured.

"Not you again," I moan.

I am in the hospital. The matron hovers around me, pulling my bed sheets tight and tucking them in.

"At least this time I'm not arrested," I say to her. She tuts under her breath and moves on to the next bed.

"Russell."

"Doreen, isn't it?"

"Yes."

"Kier's dead?"

"Evaporated. We found a shoe with a foot still in it. Not much for his family to bury, sadly. We found this though. Believe it may belong to you?"

She passes across a badly damaged copy of *Grapes of Wrath*. I nod, taking it in my hands for a second and letting it fall into my lap. It feels heavy, like a chunk of masonry.

"Wheatley?"

"He can't come back to London for a while, I'm afraid. I'll be looking after you in the meantime."

"I'm supposed to be in Effingham."

"You will be. The doctor I spoke to says you can be released tomorrow. I'll get you to Effingham and will be staying with you for a week or so while you recover from your second near-miss."

"Oh, I don't know if that's a good idea. My mother, she'll be—"

"It's your mother we're going to be there protect."

This sentence stops me cold.

"What do you mean *protect*?"

"Your stepfather, Frank Smart. We believe he's a Nazi spy."

I am aghast.

I swear. I surprise even myself.

"Don't be so *fucking* ridiculous!"

Doreen bristles at the use of the profanity but doesn't respond.

"I mean . . . how on *earth*? The man's a bumbling idiot, I don't know how my mother puts up with him, but a spy he most certainly isn't!"

Doreen reaches down into her bag and pulls out a yellow folder. She passes it to me. I snatch it from her hands and look through it. I read the evidence. It's certainly compelling.

"So, next week, he's going to be smuggling and hiding a double agent?"

"Yes. It's not the first he's brought in."

"And he's not working for us whatsoever?"

"No."

"This is quite awkward. My poor mother."

"We've been on his case for quite a while but haven't done anything because he's been pretty low key. He was involved in printing a few pamphlets and he took a journey to a jetty ten miles away from Newcastle around a month or two ago when several spies were brought into the country. They were arrested, and he vanished. Silly sod dropped his rations book."

"You're pulling my leg."

"He'd still be a secret to us now if it wasn't for that. He brought in someone two weeks ago."

"And nobody thought to tell me?"

"It was mulled over and decided against. We, I mean you, have had bigger things to deal with."

"Very well. Can you get a typewriter sent to where we'll be staying."

"Yes, why?"

"I want to try my hand at writing."

"Not about all of this, I hope," Doreen says, her face stern. "Official Secrets Act."

"No. I want to simply try my hand at a bit of fiction. Nice things. Children in meadows, family reunions. I'm finding our current situation rather hard to deal with."

"Of course."

Bettina is naked. She smiles at me and slides down my body. She takes my flaccid penis in her hand and slowly pumps it up and down.

"Let's get you hard," she whispers. Her tongue darts out and licks the tip.

I wiggle my hips, try to get comfy. She takes me in her mouth, to the hilt, she chokes slightly on it. She withdraws and a string of saliva threads from her mouth to my penis. She's about to say something when the back of her head blossoms into a mushroom of blood and gristle. I scream and try to push her away from me, but she collapses and I can see a part of her brain, pulsing as it slides out of her skull. My penis and pubic hair are covered in it and her blood.

I wake. I am unable to breathe. I have an erection.

I am in my hotel room. My suitcase is packed, ready to go, in the corner. I am lying on top of the bedsheets, fully clothed. I am still. I try not to move. I try to slow down my breathing. My heart feels like it could stop at any second.

After a while I get up and walk into the en-suite. I only need to stare at the toilet bowl before I am throwing up. I retch and heave until my stomach is empty. I clean up around the bowl as best as I can and take my suitcase and leave the room, making my way down the stairs to the foyer. As soon as I do the sirens start to blare.

"Fortuitous timing," the bellboy says to me and takes me to the bunker after leaving my suitcase behind reception. The bunker is fully equipped, has independent lighting and I am given a gas mask by a young man with bad acne. I slip it over my head and sit down.

"You needn't be worried," a woman in her thirties wearing a cocktail dress says to me. She is unsteady on her feet and she reaches for my hand as she comes into the bunker. I take it and she sits down heavily next to me.

"Bloody *war*. All I want is one night out without being interrupted. What's your name?"

"Russell." My voice sounds muffled through the mask. "And yours?"

"I'm Sheila, but don't let that put you off. My husband's a Major, I never see him and I'm forever bloody stuck in this shithole. First time I've bothered with the bunker though." She puts on her mask, and it pushes her curly red hair up high. More residents filter in, mainly elderly ones. We can feel the deep vibrations from the bombing but are readily informed that it appears the hotel has not been harmed.

I decide to walk back to my room. I am not wearing my watch. The clock in reception informs me that it is only three am.

"You can come up to my room if you want." Sheila says. "My husband's in Germany at the moment. He might never be back"

I puzzle at her forwardness.

I walk towards her, grab her by both of her hands, pull her towards me roughly and whisper in her ear.

"I've never . . . copulated."

She looks at me and grins.

"Neither have I, darling," she replies. "I've only fucked."

I bite her nipples and pull on them. Her back arches. Her hands are on my thighs, then sliding up my body, my neck and onto my face. She then tries to take my shirt off.

"No." I am firm. "It's not for you to look at."

She lies back on the bed and takes off her underwear and spreads her legs. I am taught how to bring a woman to orgasm for the first time with my tongue and fingers. She is patient and tells me what I am doing right or wrong. She guides my penis into her and I ejaculate after several jittery mis-timed thrusts. I heartily enjoy the experience.

DOREEN

DOREEN IS WAITING for me at the train station. She has a small suitcase that I ask to carry for her. She denies my request saying that she's more than capable of looking after herself. We find a carriage to sit in and sit opposite each other. I am still slightly heady from my experience with the very ready Sheila.

"We were bombed again last night," I say, by way of conversation. "I'm sorry if I appear slightly out of sorts."

"That hotel has a deep shelter. You wouldn't have felt a thing," Doreen comes straight back at me.

"A few trembles, but surely you'll agree that at the moment I'm a touch . . . sensitive." I let the word hang in the air. Doreen lets her eyes roll back in their sockets then reaches into her bag and pulls out a sheaf of paper. She passes them to me.

"Our marriage licence and other ephemera," she says as I flit through them. "We're staying in a house five miles away from Effingham, near Mercy. Belonged to a cousin of a friend, they've agreed to loan it to us for a couple of weeks until we get to the end of whatever we discover."

"What side of Mercy? Effingham side or Haven?"

"Haven. Is that an issue?"

"No, it's easier, more open space out that end, we'll be left to our own devices. I'm going to be noticed in all of the towns we go into though and my return will be reported pretty sharpish if I'm spotted. Do I assume that you'll be going into town for supplies?"

Doreen scratches her forehead before she replies.

"No, we'll both be going in guns blazing. We'll tell them that you were injured and that I'm the nurse that brought you back to health. We fell in love. These things happen, it won't be an uncommon occurrence. That means I can be with you when you introduce me to your family and while they might be suspicious of me, we'll make sure that we play our parts."

"I don't understand."

"Affection, Russell. We'll be affectionate with each other. Right, as soon as the train pulls in we have to nip out of the station and there will be a car ready to take us to the house. It's fully stocked. Controlling think you need a month or so to get your head sorted and don't really want you doing this, but I think you're fine."

"You do?"

"You've had your fair share of misfortune, that I won't deny, but I think you're a tough old bird, you're certainly wired differently and you seem able to handle everything that's thrown at you. Look at what you've been through so far. Two bombings and a knee trembler."

"I beg your pardon?"

"The bombing at the hotel. What did you think I was talking about?"

I do not answer.

We exit the station. There is a black car outside waiting for us. Luckily no-one else comes off the train and I am not noticed by the station master who is busy with something else. The driver takes both of our suitcases and puts them in the boot. I spy a typewriter and a radio transmitter. He is rake thin and has slender fingers.

"Do you play the piano?" I ask as he pulls away.

"No sir, why do you ask?"

I slouch down, pulling my hat over my face so no-one can see me if they look in. The car speeds through the countryside, taking corners too fast. Doreen presses against me when we take severe turns. She apologizes every time. The driver slows down when we reach Effingham. I am too scared to look at my surroundings, but even with my eyes closed I know exactly where we are. Every stop, every turning. The butcher, the baker, the old coffin maker.

"Anything been hit?" I ask Doreen.

"Surprisingly not by the looks of it. I'm sure it's only a matter of time though."

"I'm sure you're right."

I peek my head up when we leave the town, knowing that there's miles of countryside ahead of us until we reach our residence. I try to engage Doreen in small talk but she's not eager to respond. She tells me we'll talk when we reach our destination. She does not appear to trust the driver who I feel is harmless enough.

"This will be your room."

Doreen and I are standing at the entrance to a spacious double room at the front of the house. It has two single beds, pushed together.

"No, I'm more than happy with taking the single at the back, I don't need this much room," I say to Doreen but she won't have any of it.

"It'll get the morning sun and you're pale enough. You need to look healthier," she says, a rare giggle emitting from her. She pats my arm. She goes into the single and closes the door behind her. I make my way downstairs and see that the pantry is well stocked and that it's not cheap produce. Whoever put the place together went to considerable lengths to make sure that we'd both be comfortable. I am pleased that the driver brought in my typewriter; now on the kitchen table along with two reams of paper and a ream of carbon.

There is a bottle of wine, red, and I get the corkscrew and open it, pouring it into two glasses. As soon as Doreen comes downstairs and into the kitchen I hold a glass out to her. She stops dead.

"Of course not. We're on duty. Pour my glass down the sink, please. Do what you like with yours."

I drink both.

Later I fry steak and make mashed potatoes and gravy. We sit at the table and eat silently.

Finally I ask, "what does your husband think about all of this?" I wave my fork in a small circle.

"My husband thinks nothing. He was killed in France."

"Oh . . . I'm so very sorry."

"There's no need to be. It's the reason I volunteered for Controlling."

I am shocked.

"You . . . volunteered?"

"Yes. My husband was shipped home and as soon as he was buried I put my name forward. I didn't want to end up in a munitions factory or the like, I'm worth more than that. It's worked out fine. I get to meet interesting people and take down the Hun at the same time. What's not to like?"

"You find me interesting?"

"No. I find you odd and extremely dangerous. I believe the two are not comfortable bedfellows. I have grave reservations about your abilities, but I have been reassured that you are brilliant and rather marvellous once you warm up and get on with it."

I am not sure what she means. It sounds like she is talking in *double-entendres*.

"I am not a threat to you, Doreen," I say flatly.

"I know."

"I serve my country to the best of my ability," I say carefully. "I don't know what you've heard or discovered about me, but all I care about is this country beating the Germans and defending our sovereignty."

"Ironic, don't you think since the royal family has Germanic blood running through its veins?

"I'm aware. But what do we have otherwise?"

I put a sheet of paper in the typewriter.

MURIEL AND THE MULTI-COLOURED MOUSE
By Russell Stickles

It was a boring day. Muriel was bored. She sat at her bedroom window looking out at the fields beyond. Off to the right, a view of a hill, surrounded by large oak trees. Before the war began she was allowed to go there as often as she liked with her friends. Now she had to stay in at all times. It wasn't safe, *her mother kept telling her.* What happened if the Germans invaded?

As if the Germans would invade sleepy Potteringdale, Muriel sniffed, wiping her nose with a hankie. She looked down at it. KD. Her father's initials. He was out there, somewhere, fighting. She hoped beyond hope that he was keeping his head down.

I rip the sheet of paper out and crumple it up and throw it in the fireplace. I don't want to write children's stories about magical mice.

I roll in another sheet. I stare at it. Its creaminess needles me, stresses me. I need to cover it with words. Any words.

AN UNEASY DREAM
A Novel
Russell Stickles

CHAPTER ONE

People scared Michael Monument. He tried to have as little contact as possible with his neighbours. He only went into town once a week to do his shopping. Even then he kept his chat to the bare minimum. "Half a pound of sausages, please," to the butcher. No thankyou or goodbyes.

He didn't like listening to people talking on the wireless. It would make him bristle. He would begin to feel uneasy. Waves of nausea would wash over him. As a Yorkshireman he hated those clipped, refined voices. They were by their very nature more clever than he, more educated, more refined.

Michael had a dog. He liked his dog. His dog was called Nigel. Nigel reminded him of Nigel Trevathan from school. He drowned in a boating accident when he was sixteen. Nigel the human had soulful eyes. Nigel the dog had soulful eyes and that's what made Michael fall in love with him.

Michael tried to remember the first time he was ever scared of someone, but that memory was lost. It happened around the time he was twenty and at university.

I am happy with this. I have never written a novel before but I don't think it can be that hard. The words are flowing easily from me.

"Russell?" Doreen shouts from her room.

"Yes?"

"Can you stop for the evening now? I'd like to try and get some rest. And you need to recuperate."

"Yes, of course. My apologies."

I put the cover over the typewriter and undress. I lie on the bed, not bothering to get under the sheets. My hand idly plays with my penis. After I ejaculate I lie as still as I can. I do not want to spill my seed as I sit up. I will let it dry on me and shall peel it off in the morning.

I try to sleep but it is not forthcoming. I think about Bettina. I believe I may have fallen in love with a dead woman. This is the best way to fall in love of course; you will never have your heart broken.

A knock on the door.

"A cup of tea for you,"

"Please, come in."

I am sitting at the desk, my fingers hovering above my typewriter. As soon as Doreen enters I begin to type.

"Why didn't you start when you heard me get ready earlier?" she asks, putting the cup and saucer down next to me.

"It simply felt like the right thing to do."

"What are you writing?" she asks, reaching for the first sheet of paper that is lying face down.

"Please don't. I'm not ready for anyone to read what I've written."

"Oh, of course. I'm sorry. Will you be writing all day?"

"I aim to. What will you be doing?"

"I think I'll go for a walk this morning, get myself familiar with my surroundings. Will you be able to prepare lunch for around one?"

I stop typing. I turn to her. She is not joking. This is not a battle I want any part of.

"Yes, of course. Will a ham salad sandwich suffice?"

"Yes, thank you. Well, have a good morning and don't forget to make yourself some breakfast." Doreen leaves the room and shuts the door gently behind her.

"You've forgotten about lunch then," Doreen says. She is at my side. I did not hear her come in. The sound of her voice makes me jump.

"Oh, I'm sorry, right away." I push my chair back, it tips onto the floorboards with a clatter. Doreen stands back and smiles benignly at my performance.

"How was the walk?" I ask, righting the chair

"Pleasant. Found a very steep hill with a rather marvellous tree on it."

"Ah, Boggert's Hill. Yes, spent a few summer days under that tree myself as a teen, no doubt buried deep in a book. Tree's over two hundred years old. You'd think it a mecca for lightning, but it's dodged every bolt that's been flung at it. The locals like to think the area mystical. A popular spot nowadays . . ." my face reddens, ". . . for people hoping to fall with child."

"I'd like to go and visit mother tomorrow," I say. I am staring at the flames crackling in the hearth. The wireless plays in the background.

"Are you sure you're up to it?"

"Yes, but I never want my mother to find out about my stepfather," I say quietly. Doreen lifts her cup of tea and sips gently. I place my book, *The Heart is a Lonely Hunter* by Carson McCullers down on the floor beside me. It is devastating and beautiful. It is so lyrically written I always half-expect the words to sing themselves off the pages and into my heart.

"There's going to be no other way around it," Doreen says. "Controlling will publicise this as a win. That you are one of their agents won't mean anything in the larger scheme of things."

"Controlling can throw a blanket over this. This is not a victory, it's . . . just another weed that's been plucked out. Loath as I am to do it, I have no intention of letting the bugger live as soon as he's done the pick-up. Him and the spy will both be dead within an hour."

"Impossible" Doreen remonstrates. "We have no idea where the drop off is going to be, how he's going to ferry him in. "We don't have the luxury of a ground team following his every move, it's going to be you and me. That's it and I don't see you having a magic ball telling us what's going to happen."

"I'll be able to surmise his moves from our meeting tomorrow. That I can guarantee."

"Guarantee? How? You going to threaten him in front of us all? We don't work like that. This is a mistake. *You're* a fucking mistake."

Doreen stops herself, covers her mouth with her hand as she realises she's sworn at me.

"I apologise. This kind of language is not in my nature."

"It's fine. This is a high-stress situation. People deal with these strains differently, that's all."

"I just don't know how you're going to do it. He's not going to simply tell you what you want to know. He's going to be so suspicious that you've turned up with me on your arm in the first instance. Once the drop-off commences, well - the Stour valley isn't ground you can cover in a day. There are inlets everywhere – unless you can magic a memory that you and your stepfather fished together when you were a little boy, you have no idea where the spy is going to land in. The informer's been able to give us an approximate time, that's all. Your stepfather won't take him back to Effingham as that'll raise too many questions." Doreen is exasperated.

"Trust me."

It is clear that she never will.

REUNION

THERE IS SLIGHT confusion when I ask where our ration books are. A look of horror crosses Doreen's face.

"We were . . . I never aske . . ."

"They might wish to see them, or my mother might ask for a hand-out. No matter, we shall give them five pounds."

"Isn't that being too generous?"

"No. Bring some sugar and a couple of chocolate bars. They'll know it's easier to get this sort of stuff in London than it is out here in the country."

The bus journey into Effingham is not comfortable. There must be something wrong with the springs. Every time we go over a minor hole in the road we are thrown up to the ceiling. It is a good thing I am not a wearer of hats unlike so many of my male peers. It would have long been crushed by now.

Doreen is fed up by the time we arrive at town. I offer to buy her a refreshing drink at the public bar, which she declines. It is good to be back in Effingham. The streets feel comfortable under my feet, the houses – stand-alone cottages and terraces – all say hello to me in their way.

I see a park bench. Freshly repainted. I think back to when I was a child. It was the first time I ever saw a dead body. There was a man called Robert. We called him Mad Robert. He was of the drink. He had a daughter. I find it difficult to remember her name. She was whisked away by her mother and Robert was left all alone to fall to rack and ruin in his house, a small cottage on

Rice Lane. The garden was always well tended. He had a job that paid well. He used to travel in and out on the train and if he passed you as he came back home and he saw you playing alone he would always give you a penny to buy sweeties. He was responsible for many a child's toothache.

There were rumours as to why he turned to drink. There were rumours that he was a homosexual and one night he told his wife. As an adult man I am no further to knowing why he turned to the bottle to find solace, but there it was. To see him stagger home from a trip to the pub or be chastised by the policeman for scaring us children with his wild ravings about being 'shit upon' by everyone who he used to help, certainly made an impression. Not enough to ever stop me from drinking; I always found the taste to be to my liking, but I always know my limits.

I remember the last time I said hello to Robert. He was lucid that day. Sitting on a bench not far from the town centre. The pubs were not yet open, he was not of drink, of that I am certain. He looked to be in pain. Haunted. His words, when he spoke, are strained and cracked. He is full of repressed emotion. He has nobody to talk to but me. He told me that his wife had taken their child and that they will move to Australia to stay with relatives. He burst into tears when he said he will never see his child again.

I, eight years old, tell him that of course he will see her again and that when he did they would both be smiling.

Robert looked at me, *really* looked at me and a lightbulb seemed to go off behind his eyes:

"Yes, we will see each other again, you are right. How silly of me. I'm sorry to have scared you."

"You haven't scared me, Mr Yorke."

He put his hand in his pocket and pulled out some coins.

"Go to the shops and buy some sweets. There's a little bit of money for later, too."

"Gosh, Mr Yorke, that's a lot."

"Do you miss your father?" he asked abruptly.

"I never met him."

"I know, but do you miss not having one?"

This was a question that went above my head.

"I have a photograph of him."

"Shoo," Mad Robert said to me and off I ran. I got to the end of the street, about to turn away when a loud bang stopped me. Robert was on the ground. I ran towards him, his blood spurting in a taut arc. The air had a chill to it, and the steam rose from the hole in his head.

"Mr Yorke?" His legs were spasming.

His eyes did not see me. His eyelids blinked madly.

People rushed out of their houses. One woman grabbed me and pulled me into her midriff. I am removed from the scene and taken to my mother. She wailed when she was told what I had seen. I liked the fuss. I didn't understand why I should be upset by what I had seen. I did not understand it.

"There is a lot of blood," I say.

"Pardon?" Doreen replies. This is enough to pull me out of my journey.

"Oh, I do apologise. That spot back there, a man shot himself. I witnessed it. There was a lot of blood. It popped back into my head. I've not thought about it for nigh on two decades."

"That's horrendous. Why in the street?

"He was of the drink, so who really knows what his intentions were. Maybe he just couldn't be bothered to wait till he got to his home."

"How long till we reach their house?"

"It's the very last house as we leave the town. About half a mile out or so. Private. Secluded."

"Russell? Russell! What a surprise!" my mother exclaims. She brushes her pinny, tries to put her hair into reasonable shape. "Why didn't you tell me you were coming? How long have you been here?"

Doreen's arm is resting on mine.

"Only here for the day mother, we both needed to escape from London for even a day. Got a return train to catch at four."

It is at this point mother notices Doreen. Really *notices* her. That she is older than me. She nods. Doreen nods and smiles back.

"Mother, this is my wife, Doreen."

Doreen raises her hand to show her gold band. Her husband bought it for her.

Mother's hand flies to her chest but she manages to manufacture a smile.

"Well, you both better come in then!" she says slightly too loudly and we both cross the threshold. The house is warm, open-fire warm. She ushers us into the living-room, the green sofa still as hard and unforgiving as ever.

"Where's Frank?"

"Oh, out fishing. Where did he say he was going again? Ah, what was it. Around Craunford area? Is there fishing there?"

"I can't remember, it's been a long time since I spun a rod."

"So, how did you both meet?"

The question catches me off-guard, but Doreen is on it, pouncing like a cat.

"I met Russell at my first day at the BBC, I was brought in to help type the scripts—"

"Yes, war certainly does mean there's more to write," I say and we all chuckle politely. I look at the flowery puce wallpaper; the very fact that it exists confirms that there is no imagination in wallpaper design any more. It makes me want to dig up William Morris and use occult practices to force his skeletal hand to produce one more print worthy of this house. I sigh at the heavy mirror hanging above the fireplace and I realise that my mother has no pictures anywhere. Not on the walls, nor on the mantelpiece. I am hit with total recall, the picture of my father I only found because I went rummaging around in a drawer one day that I shouldn't have. I found my father's service pistol and a medal in a faded box whose squeaky hinge threatened to give the game away when I opened it. What a strange memory for me to repress. What an odd woman.

"Hmm?" I say. Mother asks why I didn't write or phone.

"Mother, you're so far removed from the war here it's almost as if you all live in another time. Down there you don't know if it's your last day on Earth or not, and if you want the brutal truth of the matter, that's why we got married. And what better to come home to someone who loves you and is there for you and will give you solace during your darkest hours?" Doreen's hand tightens on mine. I feel I can sense her pulse quicken at my words.

"How romantic," mother sighs and smiles. She visibly relaxes, the tension eases away from her. She trusts the situation and no longer feels threatened.

"Why don't we go out into the garden? I'm sure Doreen will be impressed with what you've done," I suggest, getting up. I hold in a wince as the tightening skin around my stomach tries to put me in my place.

"What a lovely idea! You'll certainly have to take some vegetables back with you. Our plot takes over all of the lawn now. Fred spent a week digging it, the pain he was in!" Mother is being jolly. It does not put me at ease. She is normally a sharp knife or a blunt tool.

We go through the kitchen and out the back door.

"Just going to nip upstairs to the lavatory," I say and I leave the ladies to it. I get to the top of the stairs in seconds and enter Mother's room, making sure that I hug the wall in case she looks back and up at the window. I squat and make my way across the room and go through their drawers, looking for anything. I search Frank's bedside cabinet, the wardrobe, pulling it away from the wall to see if anything's been stuck to it. I look at the floorboards, but cannot spend the time to see if they are loose. I search the spare room, my old room and find nothing. Disappointed, I flush the toilet, pulling down hard on the chain before going back to join the ladies outside.

The garden is full and heady. The shed is in the corner, a shovel and a heavy and battered-looking wheelbarrow propped up against its south-facing wall. I go to open the door but there is a padlock on it. I peer at the name stamped on the lock. W.M. Pinson and Son Ltd. Its dimensions are three by two inches. A solid piece of metal that I could break into if I needed to.

"Strange to keep a shed locked?" I ask mother.

"Oh, that Frank, he's paranoid about his fishing gear being stolen, but the likelihood of someone stealing something around here is less than naught. How would they get into the garden?" She points at the high walls. I give Doreen a look. I try to peer into the window but lichen and dirt make it nigh on impossible.

"I'm sorry that Frank didn't make it back in time to see you, he would have enjoyed it," mother says. She does not give Doreen a cuddle. It appears that my mother's surprised, softened edges have hardened. Not as much for Doreen to notice but I have. I know my mother better than I know myself.

We are back at the cottage.

"I have an idea."

"I'm listening."

"I am going to go and visit Frank and mother tonight."

"The purpose being?"

"To extract."

"In front of your mother?"

"If needs be. The war is bigger than her. I'll need you there with me."

"Of course."

"What I'll do will be horrendous to be a part of."

"Your mother?"

"If I have to, yes. If she merely witnesses she'll be changed forever. But the war is bigger than her, bigger than us all."

"Are you going to kill Frank?"
I do not answer.

NOSE

THE DOOR OPENS. It is my mother. She is confused.

"What are you doing back here? Did you miss your train?"

I dump my bag at the door, grab her shoulder, spin her around and push her into Doreen who clamps her hand over her mouth. I cut the phone line and take my much-loathed gun out from its holster and go through to the living-room. The wireless is on. Frank is reading his newspaper. He looks up at me and his face falls.

"Get up. Place the newspaper on the floor."

He does as he is told.

"What are you doing, Russell," he asks gently. He is composed. Settled already.

"You'll find out. Through to the dining room. Please." I train the gun on him and I circle slowly, giving him space to walk through. I enter behind him, the gun ready to take out the bottom of his skull.

Mother is already tied to a chair, her hands fashioned tightly against the chair legs. She is forehead down on the table.

"Russell, this isn't needed. Are you in trouble? Your mother and I will help you out, whatever you need," he continues. I let him speak.

"Sit on the chair please. Doreen, tie his hands to the legs."

Doreen does as she is told. Frank does not need to bend his body as he is tall enough.

I sit on one of the chairs. Mother is to the left of me, Frank straight ahead. He does not take his eyes off me.

"Mother, Frank is a spy."

A sob catches in her chest.

"It's not true, Elizabeth. *Your son* is the spy." His voice is unwavering. He is good. But I am better.

"Doreen, can you get the iron wash tub in the scullery and fill it up with water and drag it out into the garden," I ask.

"Yes, of course."

I go back to the front door to get my bag. I can hear Frank say, "your son has gone insane. He'll hang for this." I grin, really grin.

I go back into the dining room and sit down again.

"Frank, I'll give you one more chance. I want you to tell me everything about Klaus. We know that he's coming into the country in a few days, we just want you to tell us what happens to him once you meet him off the boat."

Frank's eyelids flutter. Ah, slight panic. Excellent. A deep breath. He is calm again. I reach into my inside pocket and bring out Frank's ration book. I place it in front of him.

"You dropped this when you brought in Herr Rodzen. You've been extremely sloppy, but you have a chance to make things easy on you. We know *everything*."

Frank closes his eyes and he smiles.

"Not everything, otherwise you wouldn't be doing this."

"Frank? Frank?" Mother says, her head pressed down on the table.

"You'll get nothing from me," he says.

"I was hoping that would be your answer. And mother? Is she involved?"

"No. The stupid bitch knows nothing."

This stings but I swallow it down like a tough piece of stewing beef.

"You can untie mother," I say to Doreen. I don't like using her as my dogsbody, but Frank has to know that I have complete control. That my orders are followed.

Once that is done, mother lifts up her head and stares at Frank. "You're a Nazi?" she asks.

"No, merely sympathetic to their cause."

"That's the same thing."

"Mother, you can either stay or go through to the lounge. Whatever you do you will hear Frank scream and plead for his life. If you leave the house Doreen will have no option but to shoot you. Do you understand?"

"You wouldn't."

"I would rather you survive the night, Mother."

Mother stays where she is.

"Let's see what you've got then, boy, it's a strange way to make up for all the times I corrected your behaviour," Frank sneers. He is trying to belittle me.

Doreen steps in behind him. She has already been prepped for this moment.

"Head."

She grabs hold of Frank's head firmly.

I take a box of matches out, remove and light one. The flame bursts to life. I put the head of the match up Frank's left nostril. It singes the hair there and burns. He lets out a yell of pain and tries to wrench his body free. I take the match and blow it out.

I light another match. His eyes widen like those of a frightened horse. He tries to pull his head back. Doreen is firm. I do the same to the other nostril. Frank manages not to make a noise this time.

"Release."

Tears stream down Frank's face.

Mother gets up.

"I shall take myself next door."

"Very well, mother."

"Head."

I spark up another match and burn the eyelashes of his right eye. He screams as they sizzle. The stench is quite repulsive.

"Release."

Doreen looks at me blankly. I want to make love to her.

"Now, Frank, we've been at this only a minute and I think we've discovered that you're not cut out for this type of thing, but I certainly am. Would you like to talk?"

"You're going to have to try harder than this to hurt an old man," he says defiantly. His right eye is closed and weeping.

I grab the chair, tip it back and drag him out of the dining-room.

"Bring my bag," I call to Doreen. I drag Fred over the tiled floor of the kitchen and bump him down the outside step and across to where the tub of water is. Doreen places the bag by the back door and goes in to be with Mother.

I retrieve my bag and from it I bring a smaller, wax bag. I open that and dump the contents into the tub.

"Carbolic shavings. I bought a couple of bars of soap the other day and spent the night whittling them down," I explain cheerily. I froth the water up into a bubbly lather.

I stand behind the chair and with a knife reach down and slice one hand free.

"Try anything and you'll have your lung punctured," I advise as I cut his other hand free. He immediately tends to his burnt eye.

"On your knees."

He complies. I smack him on the back as hard as I can with my open palm. It winds him instantly. I grab his head by the hair and force his head into the soapy water. He manages to get one hand on the rim of the tub and thrashes frantically as he tries to survive. I pull back after a second or two and leave him lying on the grass as he fights for breath.

I have no real knowledge if this will kill him but it is interesting to see how his body reacts.

I sit on the chair and cross my legs.

Frank takes in deep *whoops* of breath. I have an idea and go to him and fish around his pockets until I find the key to the shed. I unlock the padlock, drop it to the ground and open the shed door. I can just see into the gloomy space. I walk into the house and ask Mother to bring out a lamp. On my return Frank is on his hands and knees.

"Do we have a transmitter here, Frank?"

He doesn't answer me as he tries to regain rhythm to his breathing.

"How close is he?" Doreen asks. We are both drinking tea in the kitchen. Frank is on the grass. The soles of his bound feet are blackened and burnt from where I held matches. He is gagged lest his screams carry, which I don't think is an issue as the wind is blowing the wrong way but one can't be too careful.

"He's held out longer than I imagined he would. I'm impressed actually. He really doesn't want to let his German buddies down."

"How much of this is you trying to get him to break and how much is it you having fun?" Doreen remonstrates. Maybe making love to her is off the cards. She blows so hot and cold it's quite hard to keep up.

"Very well, let's break him now. Put a poker in the fire, bring it to me when it's red hot."

Doreen looks at me in dawning horror.

"Yes, I will put it up his anus," I say quietly, putting my finger to my lips. "I don't want him to hear just in case he tries to wriggle away."

I put down my cup of tea and go upstairs to find Mother who has taken herself to bed.

"Why have you done it here son, you've ruined this house."

"This house has never been a home. You'll find another. And the reason it was done here is that we don't have time to take him away and work on him. He's betraying our country as we speak."

I walk out of the garden with the glowing poker in my hands. The evening is darkening quickly so it gives it a more menacing effect, almost supernatural. Doreen follows me and crouches by Frank.

"Legend has it that Edward the Second was murdered with a red hot poker inserted into his anus. Now, I've had enough of you and I don't mind the residents of Effingham hearing you scream as we find out how long it will take for you to die."

Frank breaks.

Frank has told us everything we need to know. I remove all of his papers, transmitter and receiver from the shed. Mother is in the lounge. Frank is now upstairs in the master bedroom, his throat slit by his straight-razor. It is the easiest way to make him bleed out.

"Mother, we have to burn this house down now and leave. You can choose to stay here as it burns and I will mourn you. I love you, but this is the way it's got to be. Or you can walk into town and say that Frank's gone crazy."

The walk into Effingham is pleasant. Every so often I can smell a wisp of smoke as it blows in our direction.

"I think I'm going to leave service after this," Doreen tells me.

"Because of tonight?"

"Yes, I've never met such a cruel person as you before. I can't begin to imagine what you'll do after all of this is over."

"I don't understand."

"Men like you will need an outlet."

"No, I don't think so. I'll be able to turn this off quite easily. It's work. And when the work is done I'll go onto the next thing."

Doreen laughs sceptically.

"Children's writing? Trying to make it as an author? I think you'll spend the next decade living with your mother before taking the easy way out."

"Are you coming back to the cottage?"

"No. I'm going to phone Controlling and have them send a car."

"I'm not going to hurt you, Doreen. I promise."

"Russell, the very thought of spending one more night under that roof makes my skin crawl."

"But what about Klaus? Don't you want to be there when we get him? You're part of this, at least see it through to the very end."

THE VERY END

I AM STANDING up in a hole I dug the night before. I have not moved. I am covered in clods of lichen and moss, leaves and twigs. I am invisible to the naked eye. There is just enough room for me to urinate at my feet. I have not eaten and have taken appropriate medicine to stop me defecating.

I peer down rifle sights and look at the boat slowly coming in. Klaus is wearing a black jumper. His face is that of a fox, sly. His eyes dart this way and that. The only other person on the boat is the one rowing him in. They pull into the cove, the boat crunching against the gravel. Klaus steps off of the boat and is met by the agent masquerading as my stepfather. He puts an arm around his shoulder and brings him up the embankment. They speak together in German. Klaus laughs. I am too far away to decipher what they are saying. The boat that dropped Klaus off slowly pulls away. Klaus stops, pulls out a pistol and shoots the rower in the head. He then does the same to the agent. The rower slumps, but his last row takes the boat lazily out of the inlet.

I take a deep breath.

I look down the sight of my rifle. I have Klaus dead centre. I fire. The gun barks. Klaus spills back, falls against a tree, holds himself steady. He coughs. A glut of blood vomits from his mouth.

"Nein!" he sighs incredulously.

Wisps of smoke bloom from his chest. He falls down hard on his bottom. He lifts his gun arm up but it drops uselessly. Another spurt of blood erupts from his mouth. His face is shining with panic.

It is time for me to make my entrance. I put my foot on the ledge I made and heft myself up. The lichen monster crawls. Klaus sees me inch towards him. He tries to lift up his gun arm again. He is unable to. The ragged hole in his chest makes a terrible noise as he breathes.

"Who are you?" he asks, his English perfect. His eyes are wide, but they are already starting to dim.

"I am your enemy."

I stand up and place the rifle at my feet. I start ripping off my camouflage as I walk towards him.

"There was a story my mother told me when my father died. He fell at Ypres, took a bullet to the eye. Went down hard and fell on top of one of his best friends, breaking his neck. Private Percival Newton his name was. He survived the war but his neck was set funny and he would always scare the children because he looked at them at this odd angle. But never me. I was never scared of him because he was the one who caught my daddy. If it wasn't for him, daddy would have been left to rot in the mud. He fished in my daddy's eye for the bullet that killed him. I have that bullet to this day. Percival and my mother had an affair, a brief one. It produced one child who died at a day old. They both wept, but after that day they never saw each other again. A ghastly affair that was only tempered by one thing."

"Which was?" His breathing is slowing down.

"Me. Me. I was the reminder that came in the middle of everything and to my mother, she realised she was trying to cauterise an open wound with simple, carnal measures. Percival realised this, he had fallen very hard for Mother by this point and could see no way of trying to rescue the situation and making an honest woman out of her. So he left, never to return. Broke her heart. She blamed me for coming in between her and the life she wanted to lead. And I did it again, just the other day there."

I look at Klaus. He is dead. I have talked him to death.

"I really wanted to be able to let you go," I continue. "More than anything. You could go and be a spy, go to your bolthole, put on the kettle and make yourself a cup of tea and that would be the end of your day. And I would come and get you tomorrow. That was the gift I was going to give you," I finish.

"Stickles, there's a good chap, sit down, how was your holiday?" Wing Commander Wheatley enquires, pointing at the empty chair.

"It was nice to rest up, and it's a real pleasure to see you back, sir. Your spot of bother sorted then, I see?"

"Yes, all taken care of." He does not elaborate.

He drums his fingers on his desk. He looks at me intently.

"Sir?"

"You're never going to get a medal for your efforts, you know."

"I'm fully aware of that, sir."

"You do deserve all the medals and lunch with the King for what you've done for us. There's been chatter over the airwaves about you in Germany. Haw-Haw hates you. You're the man that bombs cannot kill. We have it on very good authority that several spies have asked to go back to Germany because they are scared of what you'll do to them if they're caught. You've become the wartime bogeyman."

I smile thinly.

"It's good to see that I have an effect."

"Are you ready for another job?" Wheatley asks.

"Yes sir, of course. What is it this time?"

"A nasty business, I'm afraid, internal." He passes me a folder, I open it and see Doreen's face.

"I don't understand."

"She's a double agent. We found out this morning. We don't know when she was turned or who turned her."

"Sir, I'm the last person you should be asking. She'll suspect something's up if we are brought together. She said she was leaving Controlling because of my . . .actions."

"Well, she must have been persuaded not to leave. We don't need anything from her, just terminate her. Make it look however you want it to."

"Of course."

"Oh, and before you go, here's another copy of my book. Don't get this one blown up."

"I shan't. Thank you. I'll read it this weekend."

I open it, there is no signature or inscription.

"Why haven't you signed this?"

His face turns a deep beetroot red. He will not forgive me for this direct slight.

He grabs a pen and hastily scribbles across the frontispiece.

I do not open the book until much later.

It is inscribed thus:

Russell,

Dennis Wheatley

She wakes on her knees. The damp has bled through the fabric of her tights. The noose is around her neck, the rest of the rope looped around a sturdy tree branch. She tries to scream. She is gagged. I cannot be bothered with female hysterics. Her hands are bound tight behind her back.

"Hello Doreen," I say. "I'll be brief."

I pull down on the rope with all of my might. She lifts easily. It almost catches me off-guard. Her knees buck forward and up she goes.

I have a change of heart.

I drop the rope.

Doreen crashes onto the ground. An ankle goes. *Crack.*

She coughs and wheezes, like a cat trying to clear a furball.

I undo the rope around her neck. It takes a while. There is an angry purple line already forming.

"You need to leave here and never come back," I command.

I look at her. Her eyes almost bulge out of their sockets. I remove her gag.

"Yes. I promise," she croaks.

I take a knife from my pocket and uncut the rope that binds her hands. I shake my head. I am confused. There is an unfamiliar face looking at me. She pokes her crispy tongue out at me. Her face is very fire-damaged. I can see her teeth through a hole in her cheek.

"I'm looking forward to meeting you," the strange woman whispers.

I shake my head again and bang above my eye with the heel of my hand. The burnt woman dissolves into a million flakes of ash. Doreen stares at me. She tries to move.

I stab my knife into Doreen's leg. Her good one. I begin to cut. She screams and tries to push me away. I punch her in the face.

As I leave her be, I admire my handiwork. My initials, 'RS', deep into her calf. A parting gift.

I do not deny that I am an ugly soul, but war is war. One takes pleasure when one can.

I press firmly on the brown button. A bell rings in the club's deep, dark bowels. A slit in the door opens up.

"Password."

"I am the remains that won't stay in their grave."

The slit is sealed shut, the door opens.

I trot down the stairs.

"Mr Stickles, your first visit alone?"

"Yes, you'll have heard about—"

"Mr Keir, yes. Our condolences."

I reach into my briefcase and bring out the burnt and tattered copy of *The Grapes of Wrath*.

"Here's the book I borrowed. Nearly a direct hit."

The barmaid behind the bar laughs heartily.

"Have that one on us. We shall order another copy in. What would you like to drink?"

"Whatever the house decides."

Once my drink is poured, I lift up my glass.

"Spies, may they continue to bless our country with their incompetence."

The barmaid knocks back her drink. She is smiling at me.

I smile back.

My postcard is brief:

25.04.42

Mother,

London as crazy as ever. Will be coming to Effingham for a short break. Not work related. Hope the new lodgings are comfortable.

Your son,

Russell

"Among the minor skills I have acquired during fifty years of intelligence and security work for Britain is a capacity for remaining unsurprised in the face of startling events, encounters, personalities and predicaments."
—Alexander Scotland,
The London Cage

AFTERWORD

JOHNNY MAINS

THE CUT ORIGINALLY came about because of my growing fascination with Robert Aickman's work for the Inland Waterways Association and his relationship with Elizabeth Jane Howard and the 'baby' they had together, a collection of ghost stories called *We are for the Dark*. I wanted to write a novella exploring their time together.

Ray Russell of Tartarus Press kindly gave me copies of Aickman's two autobiographies, *The Attempted Rescue* and *The River Runs Uphill*. I was completely staggered by how odd and quite repulsive Aickman came across and how he didn't seem to be aware of, or even *care* that his *own* words were the noose he was using to hang himself with. Reading Elizabeth Jane Howard's remarkable autobiography *Slipstream* sadly reinforced the picture painted of Aickman as a deeply unpleasant, controlling and bitter man. I also purchased a copy of *Race Against Time* by David Bolton, *the* book to read if you want to discover more about the formation of the IWA and the falling out between Aickman and his co-founder LTC Rolt (himself the author of the superlative collection *Sleep No More*) – and afterwards I simply lost all enthusiasm in the project. Elizabeth Jane Howard had been put through enough in real life, I did not want to put her through any more in my fiction. I think the story of Aickman and Howard still needs to be told, but it has to be done using cold, hard facts. To obfuscate (a mechanism he regularly used in his fiction) lets Robert Fordyce Aickman off the hook.

I had, however, already written about 500 words in the past tense with Aickman as the main character and I knew that those words were good and I really didn't want to lose them. I changed the tense to present continuous and Robert became Russell (in honour of Ray Russell, though please note my character is nothing like Ray in real life whatsoever) and all of a sudden Russell Stickles' voice was instantly there. Deep traces of Aickman remain, but the more I think of him the more I see shades of other damaged characters (albeit fictional) shine through such as George Harvey Bone, Tom Ripley and George Smiley. Russell is, however, very much his own man. And a very strange one at that.

It was a risk, and quite a major one, in introducing Emilia in the present continuous with her own staggered chapters, but the more I wrote the more I felt that the risk had paid off. I could have taken the easy option and have turned *The Cut* into a long short story or even a novelette, but this is a tale where risk-taking was mandatory. I also feel that the reader should be allowed to take those risks along with the writer, so if it means having to do a *little* more work for the reward – it can only be for the good. I have never written anything as experimental like this before and I don't know if I ever will again.

Robert Aickman, of course, appears as a supporting character and plays a benign role in the last part of the novella. I scrapped a lengthy 4k section where he and Emilia become romantically entangled behind Russell's back, however this simply didn't ring true so I regretfully deleted it. But it was nice to discover that Robert wanted his voice heard after all.

The Cut is the quickest thing I have ever written. The first 12,000 words were put down in two days. That the whole thing appears to be consistently decent will forever amaze me.

CHOKE

The idea for *Choke* came when doing the second draft of *The Cut* as I excised around 1,000 words from the finale. Those words were a loose end I wanted tied up; the random theft Stickles carried out at Bondham Church. In the novella, which I wrote as an epilogue, Monroe catches Stickles going back for the booty two years after the events and once caught, Stickles lets his mask slip and kills Monroe, his wife and the Reverend. It didn't work and if truth be told, felt tacked on. I didn't want to lose what I felt to be a perfect bookend and I knew that whatever sequel that happened wouldn't be novella-length. And it wasn't. The first draft was a perfect 5,000 words and I went straight onto writing *A Man At War*. When *A Man At War* ended up being a novella I knew that *Choke* had to be expanded. I just couldn't find a decent storyline for it. That came one day when I was in the shower, where all of my ideas seem to come. Two things drove the plot of *Choke* forward: I 'borrowed' from and re-worked the theme of one of my earliest short stories, 'Final Draft', where a *Pan Book of Horror Stories* fan tracks down an author from the original series. I also owe a massive debt to Stephen Volk's masterwork *Whitstable* which proved that having an elderly protagonist going up against a younger, dangerous force can be done without feeling false. All of this coalesced in my mind and while it took a little longer to write this bookend, I feel *Choke* is the right and satisfactory conclusion to Stickles' twilight years.

A MAN AT WAR

Although this is the first story concerning the very strange Russell Stickles, it is the last to be read in the book. I had no story, no plotline when I began, I simply began to write to see if Russell had anything to say to me. This is the most important story in the trilogy as it gives his beginnings and gives meaning to who he would become in *The Cut* and *Choke*. I started with the postcard and just wrote simply to see where I would end up. I have to hold my hands up and say that I have bended the happenings in London during WWII a great deal. Dennis Wheatley was indeed a part of the London Controlling Section and I have probably given him more credit than he deserves for his role. From the horses mouth: *'I was undoubtedly highly incompetent in the matter of staff duties. I took long lunches from which, at times, I returned slightly tight. I spent hours coffee-housing with my friends in the mess and the Air Ministry. I was lazy and indifferent about all minor problems to do with deception.*

I have also made the LCS complicit in the sanction of torture – this is only to serve the narrative drive of the story. Alexander Paterson Scotland OBE and the 'London Cage' also existed and whilst there were allegations of torture under his watch there, Scotland's book, *London Cage* (Evans Brothers Ltd, 1957) explicitly denies this.

After much consideration I believe his account to be full of holes and have used the London Cage as I see fit. I must also thank Al Murray for advice about German bomb drops and the precision/randomness of them.

As *A Man at War* is a fictional story with some warped elements of non-fiction running through it, please take it with a pinch of salt, but know that its intentions are pure. It's meant to entertain, which I think it does rather admirably.

Below is a list of music I listened to while writing my trilogy of novellas – some albums were more successful than others in getting me into the place my mind needed to be. Art Garfunkel's *Fate For Breakfast*, for instance, now lives in the bin. I played Scott Walker's *3* more than any other album, I found it the best to instantly transport me to the mindset of Russell Stickles.

MUSIC LISTENED TO WHILE WRITING
THE CUT

Leonard Cohen - *So Long, Marianne*
Miles Davis - *The Very Best Of*
Pink Floyd - *The Final Cut*
Art Garfunkel - *Fate For Breakfast*
Woody Guthrie - *Original Folk*
Chris Isaak - *Wicked Game*
John Martyn - *Solid Air*
Joni Mitchell - *Blue*
Harry Nilsson - *Everybody's Talkin' - The Very Best of Harry Nilsson*
Radiohead - *Kid A*
Frank Sinatra - *Duets*

Phil Spector - *Phil Spector's Wall of Sound Retrospective*
Dusty Springfield - *The Dusty Springfield Story*
Kay Starr - *Collectors Series*
U2 - *Zooropa*
Various - *Music From the Motion Picture Eyes Wide Shut*
Scott Walker - *3*
Scott Walker - *4*

MUSIC LISTENED TO WHILE WRITING
CHOKE

Fairground Attraction - *The First of a Million Kisses*
Nick Cave - *From Her to Eternity*
Biffy Clyro - *Only Revolutions*
Leonard Cohen - *You Want It Darker*
Neil Diamond - *Home Before Dark*
Bob Dylan - *Rough and Rowdy Ways/Murder Most Foul*
Holly Johnson - *Blast*
Madonna - *Ultra Rare Trax Vol 2*
Radiohead - *OK Computer*
The Boomtown Rats - *Greatest Hits*
The Smiths - *The Queen is Dead*
Suede - *Dog Man Star*
Supertramp - *Retrospectacle*
Scott Walker - *3*
The Who - *Tommy*

MUSIC LISTENED TO WHILE WRITING
A MAN AT WAR

Terence Trent D'Arby - *Symphony or Damn*
Nick Drake - *Five Leaves Left*
Nick Drake - *Pink Moon*

Bob Dylan - *Rough And Rowdy Ways/Murder Most Foul*
Billie Eilish - *When We All Fall Asleep Where Do We Go?*
Bobbie Gentry - *Southern Gothic: The Definitive Collection*
Radiohead - *A Moon Shaped Pool*
Radiohead - *The King of Limbs*
Various - *A Slight Disturbance In My Mind: The British Proto-Psychedelic Sounds of 1966*
Various - *Confessin' The Blues*
Various - *Once Upon A Time in Hollywood OST*
Scott Walker - *3*
Thom Yorke - *Anima*
Thom Yorke - *Suspiria OST*
Thom Yorke - *Tomorrow's Modern Boxes*

ACKNOWLEDGEMENTS

I would like to thank the following for help during and after its writing: Jim Sangster, Catherine Gogerty, Charlie Higson, the Brown Family, Lucie McKnight Hardy, Al Murray, Robin Ince, Tim Major, Barry Forshaw, Reggie Oliver, Ralph Robert Moore, Steven J Dines, Kimberley Ballard, Kit Power, Jessica Stevens, Jon Dear, Andrew Screen and Naomi Booth.

Massive thanks to Trevor Kennedy for taking this schizophrenic title on, it's part genre, part home-invasion and part war thriller so it cannot be easily pigeonholed, so my eternal thanks that he saw that it was a yarn worth getting out.

Lastly to family Mains. It's been a rough old time, but we got through it. My dog Biscuit died in April 2021, so he was there when this book was being written. Thank you, my boy, for keeping me company all of those years. My new dog, Lilly, has taken Biscuit's old place under my desk and has kept me company during the revisions. Here's to this and many more books together, ya wee ginger terrorist.

**FOR A FREE SHORT STORY SET IN THE
RUSSELL STICKLES UNIVERSE,
SEND AN EMAIL TO:**

MAINSMAINSMAINS@OUTLOOK.COM

**PUT 'LETMEGOMAINS'
IN THE EMAIL SUBJECT**

ALSO AVAILABLE FROM TK PULP
AND EDITED BY JOHNNY MAINS

They're Out to Get You Volume One:
Animals and Insects

Printed in Great Britain
by Amazon

20779919R00150